Love in Minor Series - Book 1

Love in
A Minor

MO FLAMES

FLAMES
ENTERTAINMENT

Contact info: info@flamesentertain.com

Front cover design: LA Sky
Editor: Tori Moore

ISBN-13: 979-8-9892058-1-3 (paperback)
979-8-9892058-0-6 (ebook)

Dedication

Dedicated to Black Coffee Atlanta (Flagship)
1800 Jonesboro Road SE

Author's Note

Dear Beloved Readers,

Thank you for purchasing and/or downloading this book. This work of art contains explicit language and strong sexual content.

This is book one from a new spin-off series—*Love in Minor*. It starts with Jamin Love, the founder and pianist of Love in Minor Keyz, also known as LMK. The R&B group is signed under Derrik Carter's, BlakBeatz Entertainment. This story does not end on a cliffhanger or have any issues left unresolved; however, subsequent books will continue the stories of Jamin's three bandmates.

Please keep in mind that this is a fictional story, so things you might find unrealistic or unrelatable may be real and relatable to someone else.

Jamin and Shayla have a remarkable love story that unfolds after an unexpected tragedy. They will teach us when two hearts strike a chord, even the most unlikely duet can make beautiful music. I truly hope you enjoy this rivalry to harmony … when music and love collide.

Contents

While in the writing lab, there's always music playing. There are some dope tracks that kept me inspired throughout penning this story. You can check out the playlist for this book on Apple Music and/or Spotify, under the same title, *Love in A Minor*.

Apple	**Spotify**
https://apple.co/3ZKEqD8	https://spoti.fi/3ZLYdlA

CHAPTER 1

Jamin Love's forehead creased as he reached for the remote control. Before relaxing against the plush gray couch, he pressed the button to turn up the surround system's volume. His eyes were glued to the 65-inch smart television displaying an episode of *Baller Bizness*, the popular Atlanta-based daytime talk show. They were notorious for reporting the inside scoop on breaking celebrity and entertainment news, but most of all, celebrity gossip. Initially, he was going to turn the TV off. That was until one of the show's hosts, LaLa, mentioned that she had the latest tea on a group under the BlakBeatz Entertainment label. Listening to her now, Jamin was glad he hadn't.

"Welcome back to Baller Bizness. I'm your host, LaLa."

"Annnnd I'm your lovely co-host, Sisko."

LaLa flashed a smile his way before turning her attention to the camera. "If you're just tuning in, you've joined us just in time. Before the commercial break, we were getting ready to serve up some piping hot tea. Today's special guest used to be signed under the BlakBeatz Entertainment label and sang with a popular band we all know and love. Baller babes, please put your hands together and welcome to Baller Bizness, Brandee Green, former lead vocalist of Love in Minor Keyz."

While the audience applauded, LaLa and Sisko stood from their armchairs to greet the brown-skinned woman in the form-fitting red pantsuit, crossing the studio's stage. LaLa proffered her hand first. After shaking LaLa's hand, Brandee shook Sisko's. They waited for Brandee to be seated in the armchair on the opposite side of theirs before they sat down.

Once sitting, LaLa extended another greeting. "Welcome, Brandee."

She smiled and tipped her head in their direction. "Thank you, LaLa and Sisko, for having me."

LaLa responded cheerfully. "You're welcome. And thank you for agreeing to come on the show. Well, let's get right to it. Tell us exactly what happened. Why aren't you with LMK anymore?"

"Two words: Jamin Love."

LaLa leaned forward and inquired in a coaxing tone. "Please, tell us more. What about Jamin Love?"

"The man's a total ass—"

LaLa held up a hand. "Hold on now. We try to keep it classy and clean 'round here at Baller Bizness."

"Hmph, okay, simply put then. He's rude, condescending, and acts like a dictator. The man's attitude stinks like hot garbage. He was always grumpy. I'm talking rude, obnoxious, and overbearing for no reason, just because. It made working with him impossible."

"Was he like this every single day?" LaLa urged.

Brandee nodded. "Yes, pretty much. And he didn't let up."

"What was it like with the rest of the band?" Sisko interjected.

"Everybody else was cool. It was all him. He criticizes everything and goes overboard on being a perfectionist. You can never do right by Jamin. He compared you to his cousin. I mean, I get it. Cami was great. The girl could sing. We all know this. But how can you show him what you've got when he's already shooting you down, comparing your skills to hers? And forget about anybody having a say on anything. What he says goes. No one questions him. Overall, it was a toxic environment. I just couldn't take it anymore."

Sisko tsked. "With Brandee leaving, how many lead singers does this make that LMK's gone through?"

"Can anybody keep up?" LaLa quipped before snorting. "Let's see. I think she's the fourth singer they've had in the last year since Cami's untimely passing. And since Brandee's not the first to say she wasn't able to work with Jamin, it's obvious what's going on here."

Sisko agreed with a head bob. "Yes, LaLa, it's pretty clear that Cami's death is still affecting him. I believe in taking a break, which they did. But personally, I don't think Jamin's given it enough time. If anybody in that crew needed more time off, it was him. She's family to him. Grieving is a process, and time is needed to go through each stage until you've accepted or rather learned to cope with the loss. However, I also know because of their contractual obligations with BlakBeatz, they had to get back out there. So, I can't imagine how hard it is for Jamin to have to replace his cousin with a complete stranger."

"Neither can I, but he's wasting BlakBeatz's money with this revolving door. Jamin can't keep this up and expect Derrik to be okay with it."

"I doubt he is. Your friend is about making money. At some point, he'll make an executive decision, and Jamin will have to accept it." Sisko said, waving a dismissive hand.

Brandee cut her eyes and retorted, "Doesn't mean Jamin will change that funky attitude, and that person will be able to deal with it. The problem is keeping the artist he works with."

Sisko exchanged a wide-eyed glance in LaLa's direction. He picked up his cup of tea and leaned back. His eyes ping-ponged from Brandee to LaLa before taking a sip.

LaLa smirked. "Good point. And let's not forget that LMK was at the top of the charts prior to Cami's death. For the last couple of years, they were hitting it big in every category. I believe they were on their way to winning a Grammy. No, I retract that. I know they would've taken home a few had this tragedy not happened. It's so unfortunate Jamin's unable to work with others."

Sisko sat up and returned his cup to the table in between them. He popped his lips, "I'm gonna say this: they're gonna need to bring in a powerhouse voice and that person must be able to deal with Jamin Love for this band to get back to that level. If they don't, I'm not sure what the future will be for LMK."

LaLa shrugged, speaking candidly. "If Jamin keeps this up, there might not be a future for LMK."

"Fuck!" Jamin bellowed. He'd heard enough. Brandee had been a liability. She wasn't a notably talented singer to begin with. Of course, he was a perfectionist. He had to be. What would it look like to have a whack-ass singer in place of his cousin? He wasn't going to let Brandee or any of those other sub-par singers ruin LMK's brand. Jamin didn't care what LaLa or Sisko said. They didn't know what they were talking about. His band didn't need a lead singer to stay at the top of the charts. He hit the power button on the remote and threw it on the other side of the couch.

"Uh uhn, Jamin, stop moving so much."

His attention was snapped back into the room by the aggressive tug on his dick. Jamin lowered his gaze to the woman kneeling between his thighs. She swiped away the saliva trailing from his dick to her mouth. He noticed she still had a firm grip on his swollen shaft. Her tongue slithered out, moistening her red-stained round lips. In his frustration with LaLa and Sisko, he'd honestly forgotten Kelly had been giving him head. She smiled when their eyes met. She parted her lips and was about to lower her head.

He slipped a hand between her lips and the leaky tip. Easing his shaft from her grasp, Jamin shifted his position on the couch. "Nah, Kels."

"Whatchu mean *nah?*" She rotated her neck to the side.

"Chill for a minute, damn. My mind's on this shit LaLa just said."

Kelly sucked her teeth as she got up from the floor.

Jamin didn't hesitate to remind her. "You know you can take your ass on home."

She sat next to him in a swift move. With her head pressed against his shoulder, Kelly snuggled under him. She stressed the two syllables in his name in a sweet tone. "*Ja-min*, sweetheart, I didn't mean it towards you. That was for LaLa's messy ass. She's ruined the moment between us. Now tell me how I can make it better."

Kelly must've thought he was a fool. He'd stopped her from getting him off, and she caught an attitude about it. Jamin reached over to the end table to grab his phone. Releasing an exasperated breath, he shook his head. "Nothing really, Kels."

She tugged on his arm. "Come on, Jamin. I hate seeing you like this."

He didn't bother with a response. Instead, Jamin swiped the pattern to unlock his phone and checked his messages. The first one he read was from Derrik Carter, the CEO of BlakBeatz Entertainment. The second message came from the A&R executive, Lennie Childs. Jamin let out a groan. "Here we fucking go again. I'm over this. He might've been good with finding raw talent before, but right now, his mojo ain't working."

"What happened?" Kelly probed.

"Derrik and Lennie. Some girl went viral on TikTok, and they want her to replace Brandee." He keyed in a reply while rocking his head from side to side. "Nah, they need to let it go for a minute. And maybe this time they should let us find somebody."

Kelly seemed to perk up. She grabbed his arm and squeezed it tight. "Jamin, what if I were to join LMK? It's not like I haven't sung backup with y'all before. Remember, I did those background vocals. I know the way you work, and you know I'm a fast learner. It'd be a whole lot easier to teach me than having someone y'all don't know."

He almost laughed in her face. Jamin glanced at her for a brief second and let out a deep, exhaustive sigh. "Hell nah, Kels."

Jamin noticed the smile on her face fall a little as his phone chimed back-to-back. He scrolled to review the messages from Derrik and Lennie. By the time he finished reading the last one, he grumbled, "You've got to be shitting me."

"What?"

"She's gonna be there today. I need to get ready and go. I'm already behind as it is."

However, Jamin didn't move from the couch. He opened Instagram and logged into his account. He began typing the name they'd given him in the search field, but Kelly's ombre colored box braids covered his hand. She plucked the phone out of his grasp and threw it aside. Her face was now inches from his. She sensually ran her tongue across her round lips, moistening them.

"Jamin, sweetheart, why don't you think about it?"

His eyes went to her lips. She knew they were a distraction. He couldn't ignore how sexy they appeared, especially after she made the red matte lipstick shiny from licking it. His dick pulsed to full attention. Jamin spoke in a low, husky growl. "Think about what, Kels?"

"Me ..." She gave him a quick peck, "joining ..." She followed up with another peck, "your group ..." Kelly parted her lips on top of his.

Jamin nibbled on her bottom lip. While pushing her breasts against his chest, she moaned. Kelly slid her hand between them and groped for his crotch. She pulled away from his mouth and looked down. His erection was the target.

Seductively sliding her body down the front of his, she kneeled between his legs. Kelly jerked his shaft up and down, flicking her tongue around the head.

He heard her question in a honeyed voice, "Will you, sweetheart?"

"Will I what, Kels?"

It was as if she were speaking on a mic with her lips pressed against his thick, bulbous head when she whispered. "Let me sing lead for LMK." Then she swirled her tongue around and under the tip. She blew on it and suctioned it to the back of her throat. Gurgling noises as if she was about to vomit came from her mouth and then she yanked his dick out with a pop. Kelly repeated this technique multiple times. His lap was coated in the massive amount of spit she produced from gagging on his dick.

"Fffuck!" he hissed, throwing his head back against the couch. She'd never sucked him off like this before.

Kelly must've thought giving him some of the best head she'd ever given would sway his decision in her favor. He wasn't going to allow himself to be seduced into something he'd later regret. Jamin closed his eyes and concentrated on Kelly's oral therapy. If she kept it up for one more minute, he would be ready to explode. The sudden, wet warmth of soft flesh on his dick jolted Jamin to his senses. He popped his head up. He quickly yanked Kelly off his lap and tossed her onto the couch. His tone was stern as he admonished her. "What the hell were you thinking? You know the rules about me going raw. That ain't gonna happen. *Never!*"

"But-but I wasn't trying to do it without protection. Jamin, you've done this before too. You know, rubbing your head on my clit. I was just grinding on you to keep it wet. That's all. Honest." Kelly appealed.

Jamin glared at her. He didn't want to think she would try to trap him, but enough women had tried it before.

She crawled over and caressed his arm. "Sweetheart, please don't look at me like that. For real, I would never try you like that and disrespect what we have."

He relaxed his furrowed brow and peered down. His third eye winked back, reminding him he was still stiff as a board. Jamin reached for his sweatpants on the floor and retrieved a condom from the pocket. Tearing the foil packet open, he took the rubber out and covered his length. He stood up, motioning for Kelly. Jamin popped her right cheek. "Come on, 'cause you got my shit rock hard. I swear your ass always keeps me running late, girl."

"You know you love it. Now fuck me, big daddy." She giggled, getting into the doggy-style position.

Putting a dip in her back, Kelly poked her ass out. Jamin rubbed his head against her vertical lips, coating himself with her essence. After considering what she'd said, Jamin decided from now on that if he wanted to keep Kelly aroused, his dick had to be covered. There would be no room for a slip-up. He thrust his hips and sank into the slit between her thighs. Kelly moaned, her slick walls clenching his shaft. Jamin gripped her ass, withdrew some, and plunged deep. Moving his hands to her waist, he sped up the tempo, thrusting faster. Her moans turned into grunts and screams of expletives.

"Oooh shit! That's it, baby. Beat this wet pussy up! Make me come. Harder Jamin! That's it. Harder. Oooh fuck! Yes! Yes!"

Kelly was never shy during sex. She always vocalized how he made her feel. At times, it was a turn-on. This time, however, her loud porn star screams were annoying. He was no longer invested in their smash session, and she wasn't to blame for that. His mind was on another woman—one he'd never laid eyes on. Jamin wasn't even looking forward to meeting her. Why should he? He didn't want anyone to replace Cami. Nobody could take her place. He and his friends could manage without having a lead singer. If it were up to him, he would lay down the vocals with his crew as backup for the time being. Why were Derrik and Lennie so pressed about it?

"Ohh shit! I'm about to come, Jamin!"

Kelly's voice snapped him back into the moment. Glancing down at his watch, he needed to hurry up. Jamin cleared his mind and focused on Kelly throwing her ass back. The sloshing and slapping noises increased with each pump. Finally, the familiar sensation he sought began its descent into his groin. Pulling out, his body went taut for a moment, and then he emptied his nuts in the condom. He wanted to sit down to catch his breath, but he'd already wasted enough time fucking off.

Jamin grabbed his phone, snatched his sweatpants from the floor, and rushed upstairs to get ready. Less than an hour later, he returned downstairs to find Kelly fully dressed as well. The expression on her face suggested she was in a foul mood. More than likely, it was because he hadn't shown her any affection after their session. He checked his watch. There wasn't any time to deal with her attitude nor argue about the rules of engagement they'd established. Without saying anything, Jamin went to the front door. He keyed in a code on the panel against the wall. By the time he grabbed the doorknob, Kelly was standing beside him.

She spoke in a honeyed voice. "Hey, call me later, okay? Let me know how it went with the new girl. If she doesn't work out, maybe you'll consider what I said."

Jamin opened the door. Before she stepped outside, Kelly came up on her tippy toes and kissed him on the lips. In the back of his mind, he'd already considered what she said.

"Bye, Kels."

CHAPTER 2

"He doesn't have to like me ... he just needs to fall in love with what this mouth do," Shayla said, applying an extra layer of lip gloss to her lips. She rolled them together and blew a kiss to Lennie, who was on the other end of the FaceTime call. Shayla returned the tube of gloss to her bag right as the traffic light turned green. As the cars next to her started moving, she concentrated on the road.

"Shayla Childs, if you knew how that sounded."

"How what sounded?" she couldn't hide the smirk from her cousin.

Giving herself a facepalm, Lennie sighed. "Ma'am, no. And please, do us both a favor by not embarrassing yourself saying that shit out loud around Jamin. He might misconstrue it for something else."

"Like what? I'm talking about my singing. What were you referring to, Len?"

"Don't be slick. You know exactly what I was referring to and what it means. Look, I want you to be prepared to deal with him and his sour puss attitude. Everybody knows Jamin is difficult to work with. He won't find anything amusing when it comes to music. You're gonna have to chill on being a comedian and stick to the singing."

"But I'm funny."

Lennie raised her hands in a choking gesture. "Shaaaay! I'm being for real. Do not go in there trying to make this man laugh. I know you heard what happened with Brandee and the girls before her. He's an asshole to everybody. No one has been able to work with him other than his cousin, God rest her soul, and his crew. And that's because they all went to school together. Bottom line is he doesn't think anybody is good enough to sing his songs."

Shayla scrunched up her face and rotated her neck. "Girl, he don't even know me. Besides, Derrik Carter obviously does. Didn't he say he hasn't heard a voice like mine in years? He thinks that I'm a great fit for LMK, right? Isn't he the CEO of the label? Doesn't he always find the breakout artists? And he trusts you, right? Clearly, you both see talent over here."

"The problem is Jamin didn't choose you. With Derrik and me making this choice for him, I know he's gonna be riding you more. He's literally been making it difficult for everybody we've found to work with him."

"Girl, fuck Jamin Love and his funky ass attitude."

"Well, don't say I didn't warn you. Just make sure you call me after meeting the man, the myth, and the legend himself. I need to hear this same energy. And if it doesn't pan out, at least with all the publicity around this, I know you'll get something that's even better. You're Shayla Childs, aka Shayla Starr. You were born to sang, baby."

Shayla pulled into the parking lot where a two-story red brick building sat. While shifting the gear into park, her attention went to the black, red, and white signage that read: *BlakBeatz Studios*.

"Umm, hello? … did you hear what I said? … Shay!"

"My bad. No, I didn't catch that."

"What happened just now? It looked like you zoned out. Are you still on the road?"

Shayla glanced at the phone's display and forced a smile. "No, it was nothing. I just got here. Let me go. Call you later, okay?"

Lennie returned an even bigger smile and broke out in a familiar melody. Shayla joined in singing the hook to Mariah Carey's *Always Be My Baby*. Since they were little girls, both had been super fans of the R&B singer. The track was their favorite. They would sing the chorus to each other before parting ways or hanging up.

"Love you, Shay Bae."

"Love you more, Lennie Bean."

When she disconnected from the call, Shayla closed her eyes.

The week prior, Lennie called her with a request to meet with Derrik. He saw the trending video on TikTok and Instagram of Shayla singing the cover of Mariah Carey's *My All*. The video received numerous shares and likes and reached more than ten million views. Brandee's unexpected exit from the group came at the worst possible time. The group landed a mini-residency at the MGM Grand Hotel in Las Vegas and were expected to begin their show in six months. LMK needed a new lead singer. If the group didn't find someone soon, BlakBeatz Entertainment would be on the hook, owing the hotel a huge amount in loss of sales.

Up until the viral video, Shayla had been an independent artist doing backup gigs. If all went well with this practice session, the world would soon know she was the new lead vocalist for LMK. Her thoughts raced with sudden doubts.

What if Lennie is wrong? What if this was a big mistake? Am I really ready for this? What if I mess this up? Shayla pushed them to the back of her mind. It was almost showtime. No time for anxieties to get in the way. She took in a deep breath, counted backwards from ten, and exhaled slowly. Opening her eyes, she spoke aloud and encouraged herself. "Relax, Shay. You've got this. This is your time. You were born to sang, baby."

She glanced at the time on the dashboard. Thankful for the minutes to spare, Shayla selected the next track on her playlist. Even though Mariah stayed in rotation, for moments like this, she needed Em to get her in the zone. Shayla bobbed her head, reciting the bars to *Lose Yourself*. Once the song ended, like always—her game face was on. She killed the engine of her Audi Q5 and hopped out with her head held high and confidence soaring. When Shayla entered the building and approached the receptionist's desk, a woman named Ursula greeted her.

"Hey, good morning! It's Shayla Starr, right?"

She nodded, but before she could say anything else, the woman continued. "Welcome! Derrik said to expect you. Everybody's here 'cept Jamin. That man is never on time. And don't expect him to be, 'cept on the days leading up to shows. That's when he's here first. I sure hope you work out because

I'm sick of him changing these lead singers like his drawers. That last one though. Well, I'm sure you already know about Brandee. Of course, she didn't work out, which is why you're here. Derrik seems confident you're what LMK's been missing. I hope so. Ever since Cami passed away, Jamin ain't been right. That boy can sing his ass off too, and I know he misses her terribly. Oh wait, you're gonna need your own key card to get in before and after hours. I've got that for you right here. Usually, Hodges is here or one of his guys, so you don't have to worry about walking out alone at night if you're here late. You gone on back and get yourself situated. They're in the live room, the last door on the right. I see you already have your tea, right? Well, they have a runner. She's new too and should be in here soon. Did you need anything else?"

"No, umm, I think I'm good, Miss umm—"

"Oh chile, it's just Ursula."

"Okay, Ursula. Thank you." Shayla accepted the small, round key card and flashed her a smile.

Before Shayla could walk away, Ursula decided to share the scoop on LMK. The older woman with salt and pepper locs continued for an additional ten minutes, giving short yet intimate bios about each of the band members. Shayla made a mental note never to discuss anything personal around a busybody like Ursula. After spilling all the tea, she went back to whatever she'd been doing on the computer prior to Shayla's arrival. Repositioning the bookbag on her back, Shayla walked through the glass double doors on the opposite side of Ursula's desk.

As she walked down the long hall leading to the sound booths, control, and machine rooms, Shayla scanned the wall of plaques. It was unexpected that LMK would be as successful as they'd been, given the evolution of the music industry. BlackBeatz wasn't like the other record companies–going the less expensive way with solo artists rather than bands. Derrik invested in the band, knowing they would become the next breakout artists. Over the past three years, Jamin and LMK received awards from BET, Billboard, iHeart Radio, and MTV. Everyone compared the group's musical style to the likes of Silk Sonic and Sault. Last year, they made it to the biggest stage as a Grammy nominee but lost to H.E.R., who won with her self-titled R&B album. Shayla was equally as excited as she was nervous. She would be pursuing her passion and getting the chance to perform with one of the most well-known bands in the world. When she reached the door, Shayla took a deep breath, held it for a few seconds, and exhaled slowly. She turned the knob and pushed the door open.

Shayla was awestruck by the studio's massive recording live room, which featured a thirty-foot ceiling and oak floors. There was a large glass window against the wall with a couple of sound engineers sitting behind it. The two men paused their conversation and turned to acknowledge her with nods. She returned a nod before scoping out the rest of the room. Her gaze landed on the Yamaha grand piano that sat in the middle of the room. She knew right away it was where Jamin sat. Her eyes shifted to the three people in a huddle a few feet away, who were now focused on her.

She began moving toward them and cleared her throat with a wave. "Umm, hey. I'm Shayla."

The guy standing near the drum set had to be the drummer Ursula said was the group's community peen. He was the first to welcome her. "'Sup? I'm Jace. How you doin', shawty?" He extended a hand in greeting.

He was tall with locs piled on top of his head in a tight bun. The sides were trimmed in a neat fade. Shayla could understand him being the playa. Jace was a strikingly handsome, brown-skinned man. She grabbed his hand with a nod. "I'm good, big guy. How are you?"

He snickered and squeezed her hand. "Everything's great now that you're here. We're happy to have you."

"Hey, Shayla. I'm Daria. It's nice to meet you." The beautiful, bronze-skinned girl, rocking a curly blonde mohawk and tapered sides with designs, set her bass guitar down and proffered a hand.

Shayla shook it briefly. "You too. Thanks."

"What it do, newbie?" The last greeting came from the lead guitarist, Zayne. Although he wasn't as tall as Jace, he was nonetheless an adorable brown-skinned guy with unruly curls on top of his head.

After the introductions, Daria guided Shayla to the cabinet where she could store her personal items. When they got back to the center of the room with Jace and Zayne, they shared some of the group's rules and expectations with Shayla. The door swung open as the four of them were having a cordial discussion about their various backgrounds.

"Oh shit, look who decided to join us early for a change." Jace joked, looking at his watch.

Jamin threw up a middle finger as he strolled over to them. "Your ass betta be ready in fifteen to lay this beat down."

Jace trotted over to the drum set, picked up the sticks, and did a drum roll. He threw a big smile at Jamin before hitting the cymbal. "Nigga, you know I stays ready."

Jamin acknowledged Daria and Zayne. Then his attention settled on her. Shayla noticed his not-so-subtle perusal of her body. By far, she wasn't a skinny girl, but she wasn't plus size either. She was what men considered slim-thick. Her waist was small, her tummy flat with wide hips, a big ass, and thick thighs. She'd never been starstruck, and fangirling was never her thing, yet Shayla's breath was caught in her throat the moment Jamin opened the door. She'd watched his performances on television, but nothing compared to seeing this gorgeous man live and in color. The short-sleeved white tee with the group's insignia stretched across his well-defined chest. Endless tattoos covered the honey-colored skin of his muscular arms. She didn't particularly care for men in skinny jeans, but damn, Jamin had her rethinking that. Shayla peeped his wide gait. When a man's legs were bowed, it usually suggested one of two things: his mother neglected to get his legs straightened, or his nuts hung low, which meant his package was enormous. The latter might've been a myth, but she noticed the length of his feet too. She gulped, and her gaze swept back up to his chiseled jawline, full lips, and thick brows over almond-shaped brown eyes. His natural sandy brown locs were pulled back into a high ponytail, but they were still past his wide shoulders. The top of his head almost touched the door frame. She had no idea he was that tall. Her mind conjured up the image of a cup of hazelnut-flavored coffee. Their eyes met for a moment. Suddenly, her throat felt parched. She wanted to exchange the tea in her Starbucks cup and quench her thirst with a venti of Jamin. *Really, Shay? You have to work with this man!* Stuck, she couldn't find the words to speak. Her tongue was too heavy. Forcing a firm swallow, she waved instead and flashed him a big, dimpled smile.

"Instead of standing there gawking at me, how about you get me a green tea with lemon and extra honey?"

Shayla blinked a couple of times. She wasn't sure she heard him right. Before she could correct him, Jamin shook his head and looked past her, speaking directly to Jace. "Why do they hire these girls knowing they can't handle working around us? I'm sure your ass will fuck this one too, and she'll be gone in a week."

"Nigga, I swear you always outta pocket." Jace groaned.

Finally finding some words, Shayla held up her hand. "Wait a minute. Excuse you!"

Jamin looked down at her and she opened her mouth to address him, but Daria spoke up. "Jamin, this is Shayla Starr. She's our new lead vocalist. Shayla, meet the man behind Love in Minor Keyz, Jamin Love."

His eyes swung from Daria back to Shayla. Jamin did a quick once-over. Massaging his chin, his eyes appeared to sparkle when he smiled. He wore a gold grill on his bottom row of teeth. "My bad yo. Nice to meet you, newbie. But I still need my tea. You gonna get it for me, *Shayla?*"

Her traitorous pussy twitched. *Dammit! Why did he say my name like that? No, why is he looking at me like that?* For a split second, she was stuck again, but as she stared into those chestnut brown eyes, it dawned on Shayla he was trying to play her. She came close to snapping her own neck from the abrupt and fast rotation. "Hell no, nigga. Do I look like the runner to you? I came here to sang. Get somebody else to do it."

Daria snorted. She could hear Jace and Zayne chuckling behind her. Jamin stared at her for a few more seconds. Without another word, he huffed and walked over to the grand piano. Once he sat down, he played a few chords. Shayla pressed her lips together, cutting her eyes at him. She did a few breathing exercises to center herself.

Jace came over. He spoke low where only she could hear. "Don't let him get to you, newbie. Do like you 'posed to do. Blow his ass away. 'Cause you were born to sang, baby."

Shayla raised a brow at him but nodded.

Jace clapped his hands and spoke in a boisterous tone, "A'ight, newbie, today it's about getting familiar with your style. We're gonna do a few covers. We picked the songs some find the hardest to sing. Everything's on the sheet music up there on the stand next to the mic. We'll follow you on whatever you choose unless the maestro over there has a problem with it and wants to take the lead."

"Fuck you," Jamin shot back.

Jace laughed and left her to get settled in. While heading over to the microphone, the actual runner for the group entered the room to get everyone's order. After giving the young girl her order for a refill of green tea with honey and lemon, Shayla spent several minutes warming up until she heard his voice.

"LMK, it's time to give the people what they want."

"And what they want?" Jace, Daria, and Zayne responded in unison.

As he played the all-too-familiar melody, Jamin's velvety tenor voice murmured gently, "All of this L-O-V-E."

Before taking the stage and beginning their performances, she'd heard Jamin and his band say this. Shayla closed her eyes, envisioning herself being able to recite the same one day soon and hopefully at their next live event. She'd always imagined herself as a singer, performing as the lead as opposed to the backup. It was a once-in-a-lifetime chance to be standing there with the renowned band. She needed to nail this moment.

"Aye, newbie, you plan on singing today, or you ain't cut out for this after all?" It was Jamin's voice that brought her back into the room.

Jace gave Jamin a look while shaking his head. With a smile and a reassuring tone, Jace pointed a drumstick in her direction. "We're ready whenever you are, newbie."

Shayla nodded. Flipping through the sheets, she saw a couple of hits by Mariah Carey and Whitney Houston but decided on the one she knew would be slow as well as a great way to show her range. It was Beyonce's contribution to the Dreamgirls movie. She took in a long breath and released it while counting back from five to one. Even though her heart pounded in her ears, her voice was steady as she began with the opening verse. Jamin came in with the piano. When Jace, Daria, and Zayne joined in with their instruments—she adjusted, settling into the rhythm and flow of being accompanied by the band. By the time she reached the chorus, Shayla knew the octaves in her voice moved up the scale with smooth precision and seamless effort.

Daria moved next to her, and the ladies swayed in unison to the beat. Shayla closed her eyes, hitting every high note without letting up. Jace egged her on along with Zayne. The song's multiple crescendos enabled her to demonstrate her range as she continued to bellow out the notes. As they were coming to the end of the song, Shayla held up her hand. She extended the song by singing a verse that wasn't part of the original version of *Listen*. Shayla hadn't noticed everyone stopped playing. She finished her rendition of the ballad in acapella. Daria, Jace, Zayne, and even the guys behind the window at the soundboard stood up and clapped. She raised her hands to her cheeks, knowing they were now a shade of crimson. Her nerves were shot, but she'd given it her all. She couldn't help it. Her parents taught her to 'either go big or go home.'

Jace tapped on his drums as he quipped, "Okay, maestro, what do you think of our newbie now?"

Shayla held her breath as Jamin glanced up from the piano at his crew. He shrugged indifferently. His eyes found hers. Without looking away, he responded in an unimpressed tone. "Meh, that was an okay start. Let's see if she can hit them Whitney notes."

CHAPTER 3

"Oh-emmm-geee! This has been an experience like no other! It was one of the best jam sessions I've ever been a part of, like for real. You guys totally rock! Thank you for welcoming me into LMK." Shayla beamed.

"It was easy. You fit right in, newbie." Jace complimented, holding up a hand.

"Thank you!" she squealed, exchanging a high-five before heading over to the area to retrieve her belongings.

Without so much as a glance in his direction, the ball of fire skipped right past Jamin. Her perfume flooded his nostrils. As his cell vibrated in his pocket, he followed the sweet scent's trail. He pulled the phone from his jeans and looked down. It was Derrik texting to let him know he would be arriving shortly to discuss how it went with Shayla. Jamin released an annoyed sigh and grumbled under his breath.

It should've been a normal practice session, but it wasn't. The happy-go-lucky singer with a weird sense of humor was unlike any of the other lead vocalists before her. Not only did she crack jokes he didn't find funny, but she switched up some of the songs they'd agreed on for her to sing. Shayla convinced his band to back her up on half of Mariah Carey's discography. He'd had enough of MiMi by the time they got to *Fantasy*. She disrupted their usual routine and the way he liked things to run. Furthermore, it didn't help they spent most of the day inflating her ego. Now she was going overboard about it. All of what she displayed a moment ago wasn't even necessary – the over-exaggerated words of gratitude.

Oh-emmm-geee! It was one of thee best jam sessions... You guys totally rock! Whatever.

Besides, as he suspected, none of her words were directed at him. Throughout the practice, he'd been distant toward her and uninterested in anything that didn't involve music. The only thing that mattered to him was if she could sing. His relentless pursuit of perfection required her to repeat several major scales until she got it right. At least she didn't crumble under pressure, which couldn't be said for the others preceding her. Jamin watched as she bent over to pick up her bookbag from the storage cabinet.

Damn, newbie.

"Ahem."

He spun around on the piano bench as though he'd been caught with his hand in the cookie jar. "What motherfucka?"

Jace laughed and gestured behind him. Jamin turned to see Shayla heading in their direction with a Cheshire cat grin on her face. He peered up when she approached the piano. *She has a dimple in her left cheek.* He hadn't seen it earlier. Jamin glanced at Jace, who was grinning back at Shayla. Shaking his head, he fought the urge to smack his teeth. Swinging his eyes back to her, he returned a blank stare. He watched her smile fade. She struggled through different expressions until she settled into a relaxed face and blew out a breath from her glossed, pouty lips. *Damn squared.* He also failed to notice how full her lips were.

She tipped her head, speaking in a neutral tone. "Night, Jamin."

Without giving him a chance to respond, Shayla shifted her body to his best friend. Her whole attitude switched up. The big grin returned. She clapped her hands together and spoke in a cheerful, sing-song tone. "I hope you have a good night, Jace!"

Jace responded with an upward head nod. "You too, newbie. See ya bright and early tomorrow."

Jamin watched as she waved to the sound engineers and then his other bandmates. He looked back at Jace, who had a mischievous grin plastered on his face, and was watching Shayla until she left the room.

He rotated his neck in Jamin's direction, leaned over the piano, and whispered, "I saw what you was looking at. That's a whole lotta—"

"Nigga, shut the fuck up. No, I wasn't."

He straightened his posture. "Yeah, tell that to somebody who don't like women. Even Ray Charles could see that thang coming. You need to see it when she goes, though. If he were alive, I bet he'd be happy to have her join his group, unlike you. Don't mess this one up, Jay. She's fucking amazing."

"She really is," Daria chimed in as she approached the piano.

Zayne came up behind her. "I gotta agree with them. She's the shit."

Jamin toyed with one of his locs. "Whatever. She a'ight, yo."

"Nah, she ain't a'ight. That girl can blow, my nigga." Jace praised.

Daria added, "I'm talking like Cami."

Jace waved his hand. "Nah uh, better than Cami."

Jamin's body went rigid. "Watch yo fucking mouth. Now you going too far. I said she a'ight, that's it."

Jace held his hands up as if to surrender. "Look Jay, hear me out for a sec. I'm just saying we ain't heard nobody that sounds like her. Nobody. How about this? You wanted to know if she could hit them Whitney notes. Come on, man, she gave us Whitney and then blew Adele's *Hello* outta the water. And it's clear Mariah's her idol. Her voice didn't crack once on any of 'em."

"Not once," Daria interjected, bobbing her head up and down.

Jamin cut his eyes to Zayne. "Something you wanna add, since these two got so much to say about Ms. Sunshine."

"You been down in that can too long anyway. Your ass needs some sun in your life, Oscar." Jace teased.

Before Jamin could respond, Zayne held up his hand. "Wanna know what I like about her? Shayla's range and ad-libs are nothing like we've ever had before. I like that she threw her own flavor on those covers. That's how Derrik found her. And I watched the video. She's a serious songbird. One to be reckoned with, Jay. Just saying."

Jamin took a moment to look around at each of his friends. He'd known his best friend, Jace Richards, since grammar school. The best friends met Daria King and Zayne Wynters in band class during junior high school. The four decided they would form a band the instant Jamin invited them over to his house to practice one day after school. By the time they reached high school, they were booking gigs for both school functions and all their friends' parties. The quad graduated from high school and went on to attend Clark Atlanta, where each of them majored in the university's music program. They joined the renowned university's marching band together. Once graduated, the friends continued playing after his cousin, Cami, convinced them to start recording their pieces. Derrik Carter saw them at a talent show at Jazzmine's Place, and the group was signed on the spot. That was almost four years ago. Most of the time, if not always, he trusted their judgment. Shayla, Ms. Sunshine, could sing, but he wasn't ready to agree she was a replacement for his cousin. At least not yet.

"All right, Jay, you've had all day. Please tell me she's a good fit. I do not have the time or the money to waste on finding another replacement."

It was Derrik Carter's voice that yanked him out of his thoughts. Jamin turned around to see the CEO of the label entering the live room with his seven-foot-tall bodyguard Hodges right behind him.

"What's up, D?" Jamin got up with an outstretched hand and clasped Derrik's hand when he reached him. They embraced briefly. He gave an upward head nod in Hodges's direction. The big man returned the silent greeting. He didn't expect anything else. Hodges rarely ever said much. Jamin returned his attention to Derrik as he spoke.

"Ain't nothing. What's good? I'm ready to hear what you think about Shayla. I already know she has pipes. Did you hold off on being overly critical and put that superior attitude of yours to the side so she could show it off?"

He didn't get a chance to respond.

Jace bogarted his way between the two men and extended his hand to Derrik. They exchanged a quick dap. "Hell no! Man, D, you know this grumpy ass nigga gave her the hardest time, but yoooo! He can't even lie. Shayla blew us all away. The girl has more than pipes. She came with a whole plumbing system."

Jamin groaned as he shot his best friend a side-eye.

"She sure did!" Daria came over and nodded, standing between Jamin and Jace.

Zayne moved to the other side of Jamin. "Derrik, screw what LaLa said. I think this year we have a chance at going platinum, and hell yeah, we're getting a couple of Grammys with Shayla on the team."

For the next ten minutes, Jamin listened as his friends shared the different styles of singing Shayla showcased in the few hours she'd practiced with them. Even if he wanted to, Jamin couldn't refute anything his friends and bandmates said. She was good. No. She was better than good. What some referred to as 'Black Girl Magic,' Shayla showed she possessed a lot of it. She had a powerful voice. He couldn't even put her in the category of Whitney or Mariah. Shayla was in a class by herself. None of the previous lead vocalists could match her talent. His loyalty to the memory of his cousin Cami ran deep. He thought no one's voice could touch her angelic sound. Now he wasn't so sure. A few times during practice, he found himself engrossed in Shayla's melodic voice to the point of being hypnotized.

Once again, Derrik's voice interrupted his train of thought. "Jay? I need to hear you say it. Are we signing Shayla to LMK?"

He took a moment to glance around at his friends. Their love for music ran as deep as his. They wanted someone who could understand this. If they were going to have anyone as the lead vocalist of their band, they needed the perfect representation of that. Cami was the only one who truly fit, but he knew it would never be the reality again. Perhaps Shayla could be the one.

Jamin murmured his agreement. "Yeah, I guess we are signing her."

CHAPTER 4

"He's a dick. No, an asshole!" Shayla cursed as she plopped down on her Olympic queen bed. She snatched one of her custom red Chucks off and threw it on the floor.

"Well, that's no surprise. What did I tell you?" Folding her arms under her breasts, Lennie leaned against the mirrored mahogany dresser.

Lennie and Shayla's mothers were sisters who happened to get pregnant with them at the same time. From birth, the first cousins were inseparable and the best of friends. They'd been born a few days apart, with Lennie being the oldest. Her older cousin had always looked out for her while growing up. Once she decided to pursue a full-time career in music, Lennie went into protective mode to ensure Shayla didn't get screwed over by a music label that didn't deserve her talent. Getting signed by BlakBeatz wasn't just a big deal for Shayla, but it was a good look for Lennie's career as well. Neither cousin wanted this golden opportunity to turn into an epic fail. Quitting wasn't an option, nor would she give Jamin a reason to fire her. She'd been grateful for the intel Lennie had given that morning on how to deal with the grouch. She did her best to ignore Jamin's overbearing behavior. Nevertheless, he left her feeling uneasy. Shayla was happy her cousin understood from the texts she'd sent earlier that a pint of Ben & Jerry's chocolate fudge brownie and a face-to-face venting session versus a FaceTime conversation was necessary.

Shayla tossed the other red sneaker and screamed as she fell backward onto the bed's plush cushioning. "No, he's a total dick and a complete pompous, arrogant asshole!"

"What happened, Shay?" Lennie pressed as she grabbed the grocery bag from the dresser and came over to the bed.

Shayla sat up. She grabbed a couple of decorative throw pillows from the head of the bed and propped them up behind her. Outstretching her hand, she took the bag from Lennie and retrieved its cold contents. Lennie pulled her ballerina slippers off before settling down on the opposite side and tucking her legs under her butt. Shayla didn't waste her time popping the lid of the container. She stuffed a few spoonfuls of the creamy, chocolaty gooeyness in her mouth before she began telling Lennie about her day with Jamin Love and the LMK band. By the time she was done recounting everything, Shayla needed to use a breathing exercise to relax. Setting the spoon down, she inhaled deeply. She'd allowed Jamin to work her nerves all over again, and he wasn't even in the same room. The mere thought of how he'd invaded her space with his commanding presence, the bergamot cologne mixed with his own natural scent, seemed to linger in her mind, and those bowed legs were enough to make her shudder. The sexy grouch had gotten under her skin all day. Strangely, it'd turned her on. How could a man that fine be so rude, arrogant, and utterly irresistible at the same time? She knew. She'd dealt with his kind before. They were drawn to her like a magnet. He was likely a fuckboy.

"Shayla!"

She let out a deep breath. "What?"

"Do not let Jamin get you this riled up."

"You don't get it, Len. The man thought I was the runner telling me to go get his tea."

Lennie chuckled, but Shayla didn't find it funny. Smacking her teeth first, she stuffed a few more spoonfuls of the creamy goodness in her mouth before ranting. "Ugh, and clearly Jace the drummer be fucking all of 'em because the asshole thought I was one. He figured I wouldn't last a week. Anyway, after finding out I was the replacement lead vocalist and could hit those Whitney notes, he tried to throw Adele at me."

"Which one?"

Swallowing two more spoonfuls. "Hmm, *Hello*."

"Oh, I know you knocked it outta the park."

Filled with pride, Shayla scooped out another spoon filled with chocolate cream and brownies. She slid it into her mouth. She nodded as she pulled it out and licked the metal oval end clean. "An easy home run. But then he had the nerve to make me go through riffs and runs."

"Shay, did you pull a MiMi?"

She'd had enough ice cream. Closing the lid over the container, she placed it on the nightstand. She tilted her head, poked her lips out, and gazed down at her nails before glancing back at her cousin. Shayla couldn't help boasting. "Lennie, by the time I finished, I'm pretty sure those were dogs I heard outside."

Lennie covered her eyes. "Girl, I know you did not do all that high-pitch screaming."

"Hmph, yes, the hell I did. But it was so cool. Daria, Jace, and Zayne were all for it since the ones I picked had range and, of course, were upbeat. We did the top five in her catalog until the grouchy dictator got mad and said we had to follow the sheet of music he chose. No more distractions or anyone else leading, because that's his job. Ugh! Everything he picked was either lame or boring. I bet we'd find a stick up his ass if he bent over."

"Listen Shay, the man is testing your level of experience as well as your patience with how he operates. Jace said it's what he does to break everybody in. Kinda like a hazing thing to see if you can handle being under pressure."

Shayla put her hand out like a stop sign. "Hold up. What do you mean, *Jace said?*"

There wasn't a response. Instead, Lennie averted her eyes. Without missing a beat, Shayla noticed Lennie scratching at the back of her neck. Any time her cousin lied or tried to hide something, it was a telltale sign. Shayla squinted. "Nah uh, out with it. When and why did you talk to Jace?"

Lennie didn't make eye contact. She bit into her bottom lip and wrung her hands. "Uh, umm, well."

"Len!" Shayla took one of the pillows from behind her head and threw it, aiming for her cousin's head.

Rather than ducking, Lennie caught it and squeezed the cushion close to her chest. A sheepish, reminiscent smile spread over her face. "Okay. Remember I told you there was this guy I was kinda seeing?"

While fluffing up another pillow behind her back, Shayla coaxed. "Uh huh, go on."

"That guy was Jace."

Shayla leaned back into the pillows and stared at Lennie. Her brow raised as Jace's comment from earlier sunk in. She mumbled, shaking her head. "No wonder he knew about our little saying."

"What?"

"How long you been fucking him?"

Lennie waved her hand and shrugged. "Off and on for a few months now. We met at the R&B Music Experience last year. And what little saying?"

"*You were born to sang, baby.* Jace said it to me earlier when he told me to ignore Jamin."

"Oh."

"Yeah, *oh.*"

"He's cool people, and well, maybe I told him you're my cousin, so look out for you."

"I don't need nobody to look out for me. I can hold my own, Len. And you're being a thot." Shayla joked with an upturned nose.

Lennie rotated her neck and pointed her index finger. "Excuse you? I ain't no thot. I'll have you know he's the only man who's been digging in these guts for the past couple of months. So, you can take that ho over there and address her properly."

"I am addressing you properly. You're the only one up in here that's been getting flewed out by ballers, bussin' it wide open and ugh. Did you hear me when I said Jace been fucking the runners? Ursula told me he's community peen. Ain't no telling who else that ho' ass drummer been with."

"Ursula's old chatty ass can't hold water. Watch that busybody." Lennie cautioned.

"Trust me, I already know."

"And it's none of my business who else Jace fucks. It ain't like we're together. He's just something I'm doing for fun, for right now. As a matter of fact …" Lennie got up from the bed and went over to her bag, sitting on the dresser. She pulled out her phone. Rotating it to where Shayla could see the display, she gushed. "Speaking of the ho' ass drummer. He's right on time. This thot is about to go buss it wide open."

Shayla got up and grabbed the container of ice cream from the nightstand as Lennie hurried to put her slippers back on. They locked arm in arm before heading out of her room. Letting out a sigh, Shayla mumbled, "At least one of us is getting some."

"You could too, except you need attachments and titles. Didn't you say Zayne was cute? Why don't you—"

Rocking her head left to right. "Oh, hell no! Let's not even go there on how I'm not fucking with any of my bandmates. You're already tainting the water, messing with somebody under the label." Her cousin snapped her head back in shock and opened her mouth to protest, but Shayla ignored her continuing, "And you should want a title too, instead of being a thot. I don't know how you do it, Len."

Lennie stopped in front of the door. She grabbed Shayla's free hand, squeezing it. "Shay, we've been down this road before. Not everybody can do this. Since I've had my fair share of getting hurt, I refuse to let this heart be open to any of the love shit. You can have that mushy stuff on wanting to be somebody's bae or boo thang. And I'm not tainting anybody's waters. Jace and I are adults. We move silently. I respect his space as he does mine. I'm gonna go get laid without catching feelings. My coochie twitching for some of that community peen. She needs a quick Jace fix. Now come on, let's sang, baby."

Shayla shook her head but joined her cousin in singing the chorus to their favorite song. When they finished, they embraced each other tight. She leaned against the door jamb as Lennie walked past her. "I'll FaceTime you in the morning."

Lennie stepped outside and began walking away, but after a few steps, she paused, turning around. "Seriously Shay, don't let Jamin get to you. The man might know music, but that's it. He doesn't know how much you love and respect this amazing gift you've been given. At least not yet. You can handle his funky ass attitude. And you might not need him, but Jace does have your back. He promised me because he's already called you the songbird they've been looking for. Don't let Jamin run you off from the one thing you've always wanted to do."

"I won't," she whispered, resting a hand across her chest.

"Love you, Shay Bae."

"Love you more, Lennie Bean. Be safe."

Shayla closed the door and pressed her back against it. Taking in a deep breath, she counted back from five to one. She took her time releasing the oxygen from her lungs. Pushing herself off the door, she went to the kitchen to put the ice cream in the freezer. Once she had an appetite for dinner, she would finish off the rest for dessert. Rather than going back to her bedroom, she made her way into the living room. As she relaxed on the pillow-top sofa, she thought about what her cousin said.

Suddenly, Shayla's thoughts shifted to that disastrous night in New York. It had taken a year to get there on that stage. The journey had been a grueling one, and it was well worth it. Her parents taught her nothing in life that she wanted would come without hard work. But the ride was over before it even had a chance to begin. Shayla blinked back the tears. It'd been four years since that awful incident. That impacted how she approached every opportunity presented afterward. It was why she couldn't fail this time. Taking in another deep breath, she counted until she centered her thoughts on a happier moment in her life. She wasn't going to let Jamin shake her. Exhaling the air from her lungs, she released all the negative energy into the atmosphere and spoke aloud the affirmations that would give her the peace she needed at that moment.

"I am a wonderful human being who possesses a beautiful and unique voice. I am an excellent singer. Everybody wants to listen to my angelic sounds. I'm famous for it worldwide. That's right. I'm Shayla Starr, and I'm the shit. All right, sexy grouch, throw whatever you want this way. I'm ready for it."

CHAPTER 5

"Come on, newbie. We had a good flow going. What's the problem?"

"Jay man, you need to chill." Jace cautioned as he rose from behind the drums.

Arching an eyebrow, Jamin cocked his head in Jace's direction. That was out of the norm. His best friend was sticking up for a newbie.

She rounded her shoulders while cracking her neck. Shayla held up her hand and motioned for him to stay back. "No, I got this."

"You heard her. She said she got this." Jamin smirked at his friend. He glanced back in her direction. Shayla was laser-focused on him as she lifted the Starbucks cup. He couldn't help but return the stare, but his attention was on her mouth as she sucked on the straw. Once she finished hydrating her pipes, she licked her lips. A pulsing sensation thrummed below his belt. He tore his eyes away from her.

Fuck!

He had no idea where the urge came from, but Jamin wanted to run his thumb over Shayla's perfect, heart-shaped lips. He wondered if her lower lip felt as soft as it looked. *What the hell? No!* The last couple of hours had been torment. She would reapply the pink gloss, and his dick would get excited all over again.

"Ahem." Jace's clearing his throat snapped him out of his thoughts.

Jamin looked up, and everyone's eyes were on him. He nodded. His attention went back to the keys, but he fumbled over them. Quickly recovering, he began to play the melody. The deep, somber tones of the grand piano were evocative as his fingers moved easily across the keys.

Shayla's voice came in smooth. *"Excuses, broken promises, another night sleeping alone… Can't reach you. You won't even pick up the phone. Here we go again, but how could this be? The one who said you'd never lie to me…"*

Picking up the tempo, she made it through the first verse and chorus, but after a few more notes, she missed the same one as she'd done previously. He struck one of the keys, making a loud noise.

"What the?" Shayla shrieked. She jumped back from the microphone and pressed a hand against her chest.

"Dammit, newbie! You was in here yesterday hitting them Whitney notes. Well, I'mma need that same energy today." Jamin taunted.

She glared back at him. Closing her eyes, Shayla inhaled a deep breath. He kept an eye on her as she blew the air from her cheeks and opened those doe-like brown eyes. Approaching the microphone, her small hands encircled the length of the handle, gripping it tight. Jamin blinked several times as his brain conjured up and flashed an image of her hands wrapped around his dick. *What the fuck!* Whipping his head away from her, he forced himself to focus on his hands.

"All right, again. From the top!" He commanded as he began playing through several chords. Shayla sang, and like before, her voice came in strong. She carried the tone steady. By the time the band joined them, she was up a couple of octaves and pushing them through to the bridge. At first, Jamin was lost in her angelic sound, but his forehead creased the moment they made it to the second chorus. It was off. The rhythm. The pitch. Instead of everything coming together to create a perfect melody, the overall sound was nothing but noise in his ears. Holding a hand up, his voice boomed. "Stop! Everybody, just stop!"

He pushed away from the piano. Rising to his feet, he walked over to the wall before returning to the piano. He went back to the wall and then returned to the piano. By the time he crossed the room for a fourth time, Jace spoke up.

"Umm, Jay, do wanna enlighten us on why you're pacing a hole into the floor over there?"

Jamin stopped mid-stride and snapped his head in their direction. Instead of answering Jace, he walked over and stopped a few feet in front of her. Looking down and squinting his eyes at Shayla, he criticized. "I was trying to figure it out, and finally, it dawned on me. Newbie here, *Ms. Sunshine,* had y'all fooled with the songs she chose yesterday. She had them memorized."

Jace smacked his teeth. "Of course she did. We all grew up on them songs."

"Nigga, pay attention. I'm challenging her with chords, which are easy, by the way, and she's still fucking up."

He didn't miss when her eyes widened, and then the frown formed into a cute little pout on those sexy, kissable lips. *No. Not sexy and in no way kissable.* Willing his eyes away from her mouth, Jamin scowled at Jace. "Man, y'all asses was letting her play you with those MiMi hits because she know them tunes by heart. Now that I'm giving her different notes to sing, she keeps missing them. You can't hear that shit?"

"I can hit them if you give me a chance, Oscar!" Shayla snapped back.

His brows furrowed in confusion. "*Oscar?* Who the hell is Oscar?"

Shayla jabbed an accusatory finger at him as she shouted. "You! You grouchy bully! I'm really trying, but you're not being patient! We all know damn well I can sing your lil' song. That's not the problem. You're trying too hard to trip me up with some new tricks you're playing on them keys. Let's not pretend a minute ago you didn't skip about two, no, maybe three notes. I heard you. And I know they did too. You're not that fucking perfect!"

He heard their stifled snickers. Jamin looked up and saw his friends attempting to hold back the laughter. He wasn't about to admit his mistake. It would be an embarrassment if they knew what distracted him earlier. Rolling his eyes back down to her, his enraged glare clashed with defiant, sienna-colored orbs that threatened to engulf his entire world in flames. Jamin didn't know what it was, but the frustration coursing through his body wasn't from her missing the notes. It was something else, and he found it frustrating the unknown had him in his feelings. Shayla didn't flinch. She stood with her head held high, matching his energy and giving it right back. Both maintained an intense stare-down. The air between the two got so thick it would've taken a knife to cut through it.

Daria got in between them. "Hey! Umm, how about we take a fifteen-minute bio break? I know I need one. Come on, Shayla."

Her eyes remained on his as Daria interlocked their arms. She practically dragged Shayla from the room. The way she cut her eyes from him when she looked away, it was as though she sliced through him. He knew he went too far. His eyes stayed glued on the closed door.

"Yooo, what the fuck is your problem?" Jace grilled, heading over to him.

Jamin avoided the confrontation, stomping toward the piano, but his best friend followed with Zayne right on his heels. He plopped down on the bench. Without making eye contact, he flipped through a few sheets of the music.

"I know you heard me. Don't go silent on us now."

Of course, Jamin heard him, but he couldn't tell them the truth. He let out an exasperated sigh. "Look, we ain't got a lot of the time. Y'all already know what we have to get done."

Jace shifted to the side of the piano where he would be in his line of sight. Jamin couldn't avoid his friend's disapproving eyes as he chided. "You think we don't know this, Jay? What's really up? You ain't do Brandee like this. And you sure as hell ain't do them other girls like this either. You treating Shayla fucked up because … " His friend paused before blurting it out with conviction. "She's the best we've ever had, and you know I mean better than Cami."

Jamin pushed the bench back and hopped to his feet. Before he could get in Jace's face, Zayne put a hand on his chest. Pushing it away, he gritted. "The fuck you say?"

"Come on, you two. Let's not go there." Zayne pleaded.

Jamin snarled. "No, let's since this nigga got so much to say about who he thinks is better than my cousin."

"I don't think that's what he meant, Jay."

"Don't speak for me, Zee, 'cause I can handle my own. And that's exactly what I meant. I ain't about to stand here and act like Shayla ain't got what—"

"Nigga please, she was singing them easy tunes!"

With a mirthless chuckle, Jace rocked his head from side to side. "Nigga please, why you frontin'? And you really up in my face about this? Zayne, you wanna be a peacemaker. Tell this nigga, 'cause I ain't about to fight him over the truth."

After Jace took a couple of steps back, Zayne turned around to face Jamin. "Listen bruh, you know all of us love Cami. We always will. She's the reason LMK is where we are today. This ain't in no way disrespectful to our girl's memory. It might not ever be easy to hear this, but Shayla has a voice that's better than we've ever had before. She deserves a chance to rock with us. Chill the fuck out and give her that."

He stared at his friends. Jamin knew they were right. Shayla was a powerhouse. However, the real reason he had a problem with her had nothing to do with his cousin. He needed to pull it together. The door opened.

"Are we good in here? Can we get back to making music like we came to do?" Daria quipped as she came into the room with Shayla following her.

Jamin noticed she didn't look in his direction when she took her position at the microphone. He took a step back from Zayne. Silently, he conceded to them with a nod. Zayne retreated to take his spot next to Daria. Before picking up his guitar, he exchanged a knowing look with her. Jace pinned Jamin with an unfazed stare, but nodded at him. Jamin cleared his throat. "Uhh yeah, we good. Sorry 'bout that newbie. I'll watch the keys." He took his place back at the piano. "A'ight, LMK, it's time to give the people what they want."

"And what they want?" his band members, along with Shayla, responded in unison.

He peeked up in time to see Shayla blessing him with a dimpled smile. It struck him unexpectedly and hard. Jamin's heart fluttered as he murmured, "All of this L-O-V-E."

CHAPTER 6

S hayla had been pushed over her limit for the past few weeks. At least once during the first month, she thought about quitting after putting up with Jamin's relentless quest for perfection. His former lead vocalist, Brandee, hadn't exaggerated about his condescending tones and rudeness.

The sexy grouch insisted on offering his unsolicited advice for improving her ranges. Shayla had a vocal coach whom she'd worked with for the past three years. She didn't need Jamin's extra suggestions. He ended up giving them whether she wanted to hear or not. What got her worked up most of the time was him doing it too close. Shayla had begun to suspect he did it to get a reaction from her. Whether it was the objective or not, he'd succeeded in agitating her every time. In addition to her frustration, he would unknowingly leave her aroused. Having Jamin's deep, sexy voice in her ear, her panties ended up ruined almost every other day. Thankfully, she always kept a change of clothing with her. Shayla shuddered as the memory replayed in her mind from the other day.

He'd leaned over to show where he wanted her to include some ad-libs. His broad chest brushed against her back. The scent of his cologne overpowered her senses. He turned his head to ask her if she understood. She couldn't seem to think of anything except how she wanted to bury her nose in his neck to inhale more of the irresistible fragrance. Their faces were inches apart. She never noticed how full and pink his lips were. Shayla could tell by the sly grin he wore that he'd heard her breath catch in her throat. He didn't have the grills in. His teeth were perfectly straight and sparkling white. He'd asked if she was okay.

She was not. Shayla's face burned with embarrassment. She found herself once again speechless under Jamin's spell. Other than her kitty crying with ecstasy, she simply nodded in agreement. It was all the movement Shayla could summon her body to do with him right next to her. She'd wondered why he had to be all in her space. He could've said it to her while sitting at the piano. That night, like the previous ones, Shayla could still smell him. She almost got a headache from inhaling the shirt excessively.

"Shayla?"

Daria's voice yanked Shayla from her musings about Jamin. She gasped and put a hand on her chest as she stifled a frightened giggle. "My bad, Daria. I was over here daydreaming. Did you say something?"

She held out a few sheets of paper. "Yeah, do you mind getting these copied while I run to the bathroom? I would send Jace, but he's in there with Zee and the sound guys. They think we've got a hit on our hands."

"Seriously?" Shayla replied excitedly, taking the papers from her.

Daria bobbed her head. "Yep! All we gotta do today is lay down your background vocals and bring in Jace's solo. We should be good to go. They've hit up Jamin. Hopefully, he'll be here soon. But let me go before I pee myself. Thanks girly!"

Shayla followed Daria out and headed towards the front. She handed the music sheets to Ursula with instructions to make copies. While she waited, what Daria shared moments ago began to sink in. She'd put in the hard work along with her bandmates, and finally, it would pay off. Her debut single with LMK was going to hit the airwaves soon. Excitement bubbled inside as if she were a kid on Christmas morning. She couldn't wait to hear it.

Ursula came out of the door behind her desk. "All right, that took longer than expected. This just reminded me I need to put a service call in for them to come look at that copier. Here you go, dear." She held up the stack of collated copies.

At the same time, an all too familiar fragrance wafted into Shayla's nostrils. Her disloyal coochie damn near jumped out of her panties in excitement. "Damn, he's here." She mumbled under her breath.

"I'm sorry dear, what was that?" Ursula asked.

Shayla thought she'd said it low enough. She reached for the papers, but the nosy receptionist held them away as if she were awaiting an explanation. There wasn't any time for that. She tugged at the stack, relinquishing Ursula's grip on them. She hastily expressed her gratitude, backing away from the reception desk. Shayla pivoted on her heel. "It was nothing. Thank you so much, Ursula. I appreciate—"

"Oomph!"

She collided with Jamin's solid chest. The papers fell out of her hands, scattering across the lobby floor. Instantly, Shayla kneeled to pick up the papers. She heard Ursula's offer to help, and she came from behind the desk, but the phone rang. Then Jamin's sneakers appeared in Shayla's peripheral. He crouched down next to her, bringing with him a wind of the bergamot fragrance she liked. *What is he doing?* She thought to herself as she reached for the sheet of paper in front of her. At the same time, Jamin's hand went for the paper, and their fingers touched. Shayla drew her hand back as an electric current shot through it.

She quickly set the stack in her other hand down to massage her fingers. Then she tried to reach for the paper again, and so did Jamin. This time, she shooed his hand away. "I got it."

"I'm trying to help."

"And I said I've got it."

"Yo, what's your problem?"

Shayla whipped her head in his direction. Her coochie screamed. No, the heffa wept in awe of the gorgeous man God took his time creating. He'd gotten his locs retwisted and a fresh lineup around his face. She swallowed hard. Her tone came harsher than she'd intended. "Nothing. I-I just told you I got it." She returned her focus to picking up the papers.

"Fine."

She snapped in return. "Fine."

"Hmm, and they talk about me being rude. It's you that should come with a warning labe—"

Daria's voice interrupted him. "What the hell happened here?"

"Jamin came in here and walked up on Shayla, all quiet. She turned around and ran right smack in the middle of his chest. But you know something. I think you did that on purpose." Ursula pointed an accusatory finger at him.

He snorted. "Ursula, is that what you really saw?" Jamin held up his hand to stop her when she opened her mouth. "You know I ain't do that on purpose, and I know you saw me down there trying to help her just now. I was trying to be nice to newbie. She's the one who's being rude and pushed me away."

Shayla glared at him. Obviously unfazed, Jamin returned the glare.

She complained to Daria, "I can't believe we have to work with him."

Daria shook her head. "Just help us get the rest of this up, Jamin."

"Only if it's okay with newbie."

"I don't care," Shayla mumbled. Her attention was back to picking up the rest of the music sheets.

Jamin stuck around long enough to help with picking up the rest of the papers. He left Shayla and Daria to put them back in order. They finished the task in under ten minutes and returned to the live room, sharing the music sheets with the rest of the group. Once they did some warmup runs, they began the final recording for the track. A couple hours later, Shayla was in the zone. The song most certainly was going to be a hit once they released it. She was so sure of how great she sounded and how good she'd been up to that point. However, she should've known better than to think he would feel the same. Jamin was going to find something to critique her on before the practice session was over. As if on cue, he approached the stand and stood next to her. She braced herself for his criticism.

"Aye newbie, it sounds good. But I think if you hit that note right here a lil' higher, we'd really nail it. I'm talking after Jace comes in with the beat. Then we get Zee in there, and then they hear you going up. It'll hit that much harder." He leaned in, pointing on the sheet where he meant for her to take it up a notch.

Shayla noticed Jamin would become expressive with his hands when he wanted to drive home his thought. *Goodness, his fingers are long. No! Why am I thinking that?*

"Did you hear what I said?"

She heard him, but the distraction from his fingers caused her to forget. Shayla instantly became annoyed at the thought of him picking only her to criticize. With a neck rotation, she sassed him. "Remember when I asked for your opinion? Yea, me neither."

He scrunched up his sexy face, taking a step back. He looked up to the ceiling before tilting his head in her bandmates' direction. "Yo, can one of y'all let newbie know that she ain't above getting feedback? We all need it sometimes. Hell, even me."

"Umm, I can hear you. You can speak directly to me."

He swung his head back to face her and lectured. "Oh, I can? But are you gon' listen? I'm trying to tell you how this should go. The way I want it to go. Are you gonna follow or nah?"

Shayla didn't appreciate his tone or the subtle smirk on his face. She couldn't help responding in a child-like whine. "What makes you think that's the right pitch? I was already high enough. Any louder, it'll be like I'm screaming. I know my range. I'm capable of gauging exactly how high I should go in that key."

"You know what, newbie, I'd be okay with you saying all that if you had a few albums under your belt. But you don't, do you? No. So, unless your name is Google, stop acting like you know everything," Jamin huffed.

Shayla frowned. She'd never heard him speak in a tone like that.

"Yo, newbie, I think Jay's onto something. Why don't you let him help you through the bridge and see how it sounds? If it don't work, we tried, right? But usually if he feels shit, it works."

Shayla chewed on her bottom lip. Out the corner of her eye, she could see Daria nodding. She blew the air out of her cheeks. "Okay, fine."

Jamin held up a hand, signaling to the guys behind the glass. He then addressed the rest of the group. "A'ight, come on. Let's do this. Daria, Jace, y'all get us started with strumming the chords and beat from the third verse. Zee, I'mma need you to take us all the way out with newbie." He lowered his gaze to her. His tone was firm yet reassuring. "Newbie, I'mma need you to close your eyes and trust this technique. You'll know when to come in. When it's time, and you feel it, just go with the flow."

Shayla stared at him for a second but closed her eyes. She waited for her bandmates to play. His woodsy, fresh scent enveloped her. Her breath hitched when his hand pressed against the small of her back.

"Stand up straight, Shayla. But keep your knees and shoulders relaxed. Now do me a favor."

She gulped hard and whispered, "What's that?"

"Breathe." His minty, fresh breath was hot against her ear.

Doing as he instructed, Shayla exhaled, and her pussy let out a sigh of her own too. A minute later, the sounds from the drums and strings filtered into her ears. Suddenly, she sensed Jamin standing behind her. Her body stiffened.

He mumbled, "Forget about me and sing like you 'pose to, girl."

Shayla did exactly that. She soared from the chorus through the bridge. Jamin's hands slid up her waist, right below her ribs during the drum solo. He squeezed and whispered, "From your diaphragm."

Right away, Shayla recognized the technique Jamin was using with her. She pushed all the air from her lungs and took in a deep breath through her mouth. She sang the first "ooh," and then her voice hit multiple crescendos with Zayne's guitar throughout the outro. It was louder than she'd ever sung before. She'd done it without losing her breath. Shayla's eyes flew open, hearing her bandmates' praises.

"Hell yea, the maestro has struck again!" Jace shouted.

Daria squealed, "We did it!"

"Great job, Shayla!" Zayne complimented.

The guys in the control room were all smiles with their thumbs raised. One of the engineers turned on the speaker and cheered, "Beautifully done! Another masterpiece, LMK!"

Jamin's lips brushed across her earlobe. He spoke in a low, husky voice. "Heh, it's no surprise, newbie. Everything sounds beautiful when it comes out of those lips."

Shayla twisted her head to face him. He stepped back, and she watched him head over to Jace. With his natural magnetism, Jamin had to know he could drive a woman insane. He'd left her mind and body reeling from his touch. *What was that about? Was it supposed to mean something? Had she imagined he flirted with her?*

"I told you it was gonna be a hit!" Daria's voice cut through her thoughts. Shayla laughed as she spun them around in a circle. "Girl, you just blew it away!"

"We're going to the control room."

His voice drew Shayla's attention to the door. Jace and Zayne walked out before Jamin. He stopped at the door and turned to glance back at her. He winked at her seductively, then smirked. The warmth rose to her cheeks. Shayla lowered her eyes. She hadn't imagined anything.

Jamin is flirting with me!

CHAPTER 7

Jamin sat in the spacious booth with a window, looking out at the parking lot of Black Coffee. He gulped down the rest of his tea while Jace rambled on about his prior evening with Lennie. Even though his best friend argued there wasn't more, it was obvious they cared more strongly than either of them was willing to admit. The reflection of a vehicle outside in the parking lot at that precise moment got his attention. *You've got to be shitting me.*

He recognized the pearl-colored SUV pulling into the parking space in front of the coffeehouse. Jamin hoped the driver was who he thought it belonged to, since it also had tinted windows. She emerged from the vehicle and climbed onto the sidewalk. A wide grin formed on his face. Her gorgeous brown skin had direct morning sunlight exposure, which gave it an almost angelic, natural glow. Her natural hair was styled into a big Afro puff ponytail, the soft curls highlighted her delicate face. His eyes were drawn to his favorite feature – her lips. Like always, they shined from the gloss she wore. He moistened his. She donned an athleisure outfit which clung to her hourglass figure. His dick pulsed with each step she made up the walkway. He watched her walk through the door and enter the noisy establishment. Although everyone continued to move, in Jamin's eyes, it appeared everything in the room halted around her. She was the object of his interest.

"Aye Jay, did D tell you what time we gotta be there?" Jace asked, bringing him back to the table.

Jamin looked across the booth with his brows furrowed. "Man, why you always asking me shit you 'pose to be keeping up with for yourself?"

"'Cause I know you gon' keep up with it, so I don't have to. What time, nigga?"

He groaned in aggravation, but pulled his phone out of his pocket. He cast a quick glance up front to see Shayla taking one of the available seats at the bar countertop. Jamin's attention shifted to the phone. He opened the calendar and rose to his feet while advising Jace, "No later than eight-thirty. Gimme a minute. I see our peoples up front."

"Who?" Jace asked, looking in that direction.

Jamin picked up his cup and grinned. "Our songbird, Ms. Sunshine."

"Huh? But what about—"

"Just stay here until I get back," Jamin said, walking away. He headed to the front of the coffeehouse. After getting the attention of the barista, who knew him, he signaled for a refill. Jamin approached the bar and placed his cup on the countertop. When he turned around, his shoulder collided with hers. "Oh, excuse me. I'm sorry—"

"Jamin?" Her eyes were wide.

He nodded upward. "'Sup, newbie. Funny running into you here. You live in the area?"

"Y-yeah, umm, not too far from here. You?"

"Nah, I live a lil' ways from here, but I always come here for the vibe and, of course, the teas."

"Wow, it's crazy. I'm always here too, and our paths have never crossed."

"Yeah, that is crazy. So, what you get?"

"*Bag Lady*, and when we're not singing like this morning, I switch up and get an iced *Morning Joy*."

"Mmhmm, well, I get the *Andre*, large, extra honey. And now that you know where I get my tea. I think you could do them runs for me." Jamin sent her a flirtatious, inviting wink, causing her to blush.

He noticed Shayla attempting to hide her awkwardness as she nervously bit her bottom lip and avoided his eyes. Then she rocked her head from side to side.

56

The dimple formed in her left cheek when she laughed. She playfully rolled her eyes. "Uhh, what did I tell your ass the first day we met?"

Jamin thought for a second, but it had him stumped. He tugged at his beard. "I don't know. That was what, like, three almost four months ago now? Remind me."

"Nigga, do I look like the runner to you?" She rotated her neck and poked her lips out.

He laughed heartily. "Damn, that's right. So, no chance of changing your mind."

The barista returned to the counter with her order, as well as Jamin's refill. After taking a sip from her cup, Shayla twisted up her face. "Hell no. Like I said before, get somebody else to do it."

"A'ight, see if I help you again when you struggling to hit them notes." He teased, while leaning over to grab his cup. Her low gasp was audible to him. He stopped and whipped his head in her direction. Jamin straightened his back without breaking eye contact with Shayla's lips. She had no idea it was a triggering sound. In the studio the other day, he said something he meant wholeheartedly. *Everything sounds beautiful when it comes out of those lips.* Jamin couldn't help it. In his mind, he visualized more than just gasps escaping from them. It was as if he was under a spell, watching her lips open and move to speak.

"Jamin, is everything ... are you—"

"Hey! I was wondering where you went. Jace acted like he ain't know. If I knew you were coming up here, I would've told you to get me a large *Brown Skin Keisha* with almond milk. Can you order it for me, please?"

He cringed. Jamin closed his eyes and clenched his teeth for a second. More than any other time, hearing her voice at that exact moment irritated him. He opened his eyes and rolled his head in their general direction, but he didn't bother looking her way or giving her an answer. He focused on Jace instead. There were unspoken words between the best friends as they stared at each other. He silently admonished his friend. *You had one job to do.* Jace lifted his shoulders in a half-shrug. *This motherfucka.* Jamin cussed to himself. He shifted his focus to Kelly, who'd placed a hand on his chest.

"Can you, baby?" she asked in an extra honeyed tone with a big grin plastered on her face.

He removed her hand and grumbled, "Yeah, gimme a sec." After giving Shayla a quick glance, Jamin leaned in to get the attention of the barista.

"And who are you?" Kelly questioned in an abrasive tone.

What the hell?

Jamin was about to turn around and address Kelly, but Jace chimed in. "She's newbie, or as the world will soon learn, the one and only Ms. Shayla Starr."

"Thank you, Jace, but I could speak for myself."

"It's no sweat, newbie. You the shit. I love telling folks about our incomparable songbird."

Shayla giggled. "Boy, stop."

"I'm dead ass tho', and you know it."

Jamin came back to join the conversation right as Kelly asked with a tone of annoyance, "Are you gonna introduce me?"

"My bad, yo." Jace gestured between them. "Yeah, so Shayla, this is Kels."

"No, it's Kelly. Kelly Nichols. I don't know if you've heard of me, but I'm a singer too. Matter of fact, I sang with LMK before."

Jamin had to hold back from smacking his teeth. Nobody asked her for the attitude or extra information. Kelly could hold a note, but she was no match for Shayla. He noticed Shayla struggling with her facial expressions like she'd done with him the first day they met. It took everything for him not to laugh.

She finally forced a smile and bobbed her head. "Oh, okay. Well, it's nice to meet a LMK alumni."

Jace snorted, but cleared his throat and asked, "So, newbie whatcha got going on this morning?"

"Nothing much other than running errands before I catch up with Lennie."

"I'm gonna see her later too," he proudly boasted.

"Of course you are. When don't y'all see each other? What's up with that? 'Cause she's acting like it's nothing. When are y'all gonna make it official?"

"Uhh, Ion know whatchu talking 'bout."

One of Jamin's brows shot up. He tipped his head in Shayla's direction. She poked her lips out and chuckled. "I bet you don't."

"Yo, Jay, for real. What's that about?"

He joined Shayla in chuckling while moving toward the counter. "Ion know, bruh, but I gotta grab this."

The barista had his hand up to get Jamin's attention. He collected Kelly's macchiato and returned, practically shoving the cup in her hand. He gestured to Jace with his head while guiding Kelly in the opposite direction. "Aye, I'mma finish hollering at Shayla 'bout the party. I'll be over there with y'all in a sec."

Kelly opened her mouth, but with a slight shake of his head and a stern look, her lips snapped shut. She stomped off behind Jace. Jamin went back to stand next to Shayla. She was on her phone scrolling her Instagram feed. He leaned on the counter. "So, newbie, you ready for this weekend?"

"Yep." Her response was in a curt tone. She didn't look up from her phone.

Jamin frowned. "You good? That seemed a bit short."

"Was it?" Shayla lifted her eyes long enough to answer him. He also didn't miss her gaze wandering across the room before returning to him.

"Yeah, it was. You ain't have an attitude before they came over here." Jamin straightened his posture. "Hold up. You jealous, newbie?"

Shayla set her phone on the counter. She rotated her neck. "And why would you think I'm jealous? Of what? No, of who?"

Jamin challenged her with amusement. "Please, don't act like you like me or anything."

"Yeah, definitely not. Now, if you would excuse me."

"Wait. I'm just playing. You don't think—"

"I don't think anything. It's not my place to. Look, I'll let you get back to them. I gotta get going anyway. Don't wanna be late for my yoga class. See y'all at the party." Shayla grabbed her phone and hopped down from the bar stool. His eyes traveled from her waist down to her butt. Her hips swung from left to right. He couldn't resist falling into a trance. She sashayed out the door without looking back.

Fuck! Jamin realized he would have to approach Shayla in a different setting, most certainly not around the woman he had a sexual relationship with. Minutes ago, there was a noticeable awkwardness in the air. With Kelly acting immature, Shayla had every right to shut down and feel some type of way. He reluctantly rejoined Jace and Kelly back in the booth. He slid next to her in the vacant space.

She repositioned her body and turned to face him. She scoffed, "But I thought you didn't like her."

"I never told you I didn't like her. I said she's pretty ... umm, petty and annoying at times," Jamin replied flippantly. He didn't meet Kelly's probing glare. Honestly, he had nothing to explain to her. He brought out his phone to browse his IG feed.

"Well, if you ask me, it sure as hell is giving you like her the way you were up in her face just now."

"That's just it, Kels. Nobody asked you. I know I didn't. Did you, Jace?" When he didn't respond, he saw Jace pretending to be engrossed with something outside. Jamin cleared his throat.

"My bad. You said something, Jay?"

Kelly sucked her teeth. She scooted away from him and threw her arms across her chest. "You can be such an asshole sometimes, Jamin. I don't even know why I bother."

"Me either," Jamin said, returning all focus to his phone. He fixed his sights on their songbird's profile, which had managed to get his attention. His mind was now on the strategy for capturing her.

CHAPTER 8

Shayla scanned the spacious living area where several people were in the middle of the floor dancing to one of LMK's latest hits. It'd been compared to John Legend's *Green Light* by the fans, who claimed it had a similar beat and vibe. There was a dance-off between some of the guests. While a few of them were doing popular TikTok moves, others stuck with the simple old-school steps. She was unable to contain the smile splitting her face. The long hours they put in the studio the past three months had paid off. Their new album had two singles at the top of the charts. It was a good look with Shayla as their new lead singer.

"One thing about Derrik Carter, he knows how to throw a damn good party. Did we check out this whole mansion?" Lennie asked, offering a glass of wine.

Taking it from her, Shayla nodded. "I think so, but who knows? This place is huge. And yeah, it's been lit since we got here. All these people. Is it always like this?"

"Yep, but only for the parties for his label. He doesn't do this often. So, how was dinner last night with Christopher?" Lennie paused and peeked around Shayla. She wrinkled her nose in disgust. "His clingy-ass friend claimed they're supposed to be here tonight."

Shayla almost choked. "Ack, ack … Lennie! Girl, not while I'm drinking. Why'd you make that face? You didn't sleep with him, did you?"

"Hell no! On top of him thinking we were already a match made in heaven. I couldn't get past that white foam building up in the corner of his mouth while he was talking. I almost threw up when we were on our date. I told him it was something I ate. I got the hell outta there and called Jace."

"Really? I don't understand why y'all are not a couple."

"Aht aht, baby cousin. No relationships. Just benefits. It's easier that way. No hurt feelings from either party."

"First of all, I'm not your baby cousin. We're the same age, Len. And secondly, one of y'all are gonna catch feelings watch."

"You're younger than me by a couple days, Shay Bae. And trust it won't be me catching shit, that's for sure." Lennie took a sip and smirked. "If Jace goes there, he'll end up like the rest of the men I've had to put down. I don't wanna do it because …" She grabbed Shayla's hand and shivered with her eyes rolling back in her head. "Oooh, he's so good."

"No, I don't wanna hear this."

"Okay then, tell me about Christopher's pretty ass. Where did he end up taking you? I hope it wasn't no place cheap. And that man knows he's pretty too. Did he act conceited? Did he try anything?"

"No. He took me to Palms Chophouse."

"Impressive." Lennie nodded her approval.

Shayla took a sip from her glass and continued, "Yeah, I know. And the pretty boy was a perfect gentleman. I will say he smoothed his mustache and beard down a few times too many. I lost count after the tenth time. I figured it was a nervous thing. He claimed getting a date with me had him all anxious after you told him I said yeah."

"Lying ass. That man was hardly anxious. Oooh, look who just walked in. Now they ain't pretty boys. Them the fine ass, big dick niggas right there. Mmhmm." Lennie leaned back, cocking her head to the side.

Shayla twisted hers to see who Lennie was referring to. She had to fight to keep her mouth closed. Jamin wore a mauve button-down shirt with gray fitted trousers and black designer sneakers. The platinum chain resting on his tatted chest sparkled under the recessed lighting. He smiled at the people greeting them at the door, and the matching platinum grill sparkled too. The sexy grouch looked downright sinful. Turning away from them, she grumbled under her breath.

"What? Something else happened with the grouch?"

She hadn't told Lennie about her interaction with Jamin that day at the studio or Black Coffee. She could feel it even if he hadn't voiced it yet. Jamin wanted something more. He asked if she was jealous. It shouldn't have bothered her about Kelly, but it did. Shayla wasn't dumb. Either they had been fucking, or they still were. Kelly touched him in an affectionate way and called him baby. If Jamin was interested in her, it didn't make sense to Shayla why he would have his current girlfriend around. She finished off the glass and set it on the table next to them. "No, nothing happened."

"You sure? I heard that grunting noise you make whenever he's around."

Shayla waved a dismissive hand. "I meant like whatever that they're here. You're the one that's going all coocoo for cocoa puffs 'cause Jace is here."

Lennie giggled. "Yeah, so what."

"I need to get some water and tea. We have to sing later. And I need to be ready when we do. Come on."

Almost thirty minutes later, they returned to the main area where most of the guests were. Lennie nudged her shoulder and pointed to the other side of the room. "Oh look, Derrik just got here."

With his bodyguards flanking him, Derrik guided his wife over to where they set up the band's equipment. By the time she and Lennie made it over to them, Jamin, Jace, and their other two bandmates had reached them as well.

"Congratulations on another chart-topper. I told you Shayla was going to be a great addition." Derrik's eyes were on Jamin when he made the statement.

Jamin and the rest of the group nodded while a shade of red rose in Shayla's cheeks. She placed a hand against her chest. "I'm truly grateful for this opportunity, Derrik. And I thank all of you for trusting in me."

Daria yanked her into a tight embrace. "Say less, girl. We knew the moment you walked through that door, you were gonna rock hard with us."

"I don't know about y'all, but I'm looking forward to what's ahead for LMK this year. Now, I promised my wife, Desi, y'all would be singing tonight. Ready to give us a lil' taste of this album?" Derrik asked, draping an arm around his wife's shoulder.

After exchanging daps with Jace and Zayne, Jamin nodded. "Hells yeah!"

Shayla felt somewhat nervous since it would be her first performance in front of a crowd. She knew once they got started, she'd be fine. Even so, nervous jitters settled in the pit of her stomach. Lennie must've known. Her cousin reached for her hands and interlocked their fingers, drawing her close.

She whispered, "I know that look. Don't you dare second guess yourself, Ms. Starr. You've got this. Remember, you were born to sang, baby. Let these people hear and feel you."

"Okay. Thanks, Lennie Bean."

"You know I always got you, Shay Bae."

Shayla inhaled deeply when she saw Jamin take a seat at the grand piano while the rest of her bandmates grabbed their instruments and settled in their places. She took her place up front with the lone microphone. She'd been looking forward to performing a couple of the songs from their album tonight, especially the one Jamin helped her with that day. As everyone predicted, it was an instant hit with the fans. She turned to look at him. He glanced up as if he'd overheard her thoughts. Jamin winked and threw a sly grin. Shayla looked away. She tried to shake the feeling, but she couldn't. There was no way to stop her heart from fluttering.

She heard the DJ fading out the previous song playing. The room became eerily quiet. A moment later, Jamin murmured, "LMK, it's time to give the people what they want."

The group responded in unison, "And what they want?"

"All of this L-O-V-E," he said and began playing the piano.

Next, Jace tapped on the drums, introducing the beat. Shayla followed up, bellowing out the song.

I never thought that love could be
So unexpected, yet so sweet
You came into my life like a breeze
And swept me off my weary feet

I'm scared of what the future holds
And what this love might mean for me
But I'm willing to take the risk
If you're willing to come along with me

Once Daria and Zayne joined in, she noticed some of the guests had the lights from their phones on them while others were swaying as they jammed through the song. She led them through the chorus in a steady octave, and then her voice soared to a crescendo. It remained there until the whistling finale, seemingly holding everyone in a trance.

Everyone clapped and cheered when she finished. She couldn't help turning to Jamin, seeking out his approval. He was the one who, specifically for that song, had helped to strengthen her vocal range. He tipped his head. Shayla opened her mouth, but Lennie whirled her around, pulling her into an embrace. At the same time, a few people gathered around the piano with requests for LMK to perform some of their old hits.

Unable to deny their fans, they obliged them with a few songs from their earlier catalog. Shayla opted to listen with the guests since they were hits before she joined the group. Jamin began to play the chords. She'd memorized their complete discography after joining them, so she was familiar with the melody. The ballad was about someone taking their time with the person they wanted since they had a lifetime to experience their love. Jamin closed his eyes and leaned toward the microphone. It felt as though she was being tugged by invisible magnetic strands as the song's tempo increased. Shayla's eyes locked on his when his eyelids flickered open:

No, I ain't trying to rush this girl
But 'cause of who you are
And what I want is beyond this world
There's something you gotta know
I ain't afraid to say it
I ain't letting you go... no, I ain't letting you go.
I can't, not even if I wanted to

It's like gravity, you've got a hold on me
And I'm falling, falling harder than I ever thought I'd be
And it's scary, but it's true
There's no one else I'd rather fall for than you

So let's take our time, baby, and enjoy the ride
'Cause with you by my side, I've got nothing to hide
I'll love you now and forever, that's a promise I'll keep
And with you in my life, I know I'll never lose sleep.

Lennie tapped her shoulder, jolting Shayla out of their silent exchange. She jumped a little as a reflex.

"Somebody's acting like a skittish cat." Her cousin teased.

"Shut up."

"Hello, Shayla. Not only do you sing beautifully, you look absolutely stunning tonight," Christopher spoke in a rich, baritone voice. He held out his hand.

Shayla would gladly take the compliment. The little black dress fit her like a glove, but the attention-grabbing feature was the thigh-high split with the butterfly gemstone at the opening. She peered up at the strikingly handsome man with light yellow-brown skin and thick, endless dark curls on his head. His goatee perfectly framed his chiseled jawline. Christopher was the epitome of a pretty boy. Shayla blushed and placed her small hand in the palm of his larger, smooth hand. He raised it to brush a kiss on the back of her hand. Then he offered a glass of wine. They weren't planning to sing anymore for the night, so she happily accepted it.

"How about y'all come over here with us?" his friend suggested.

Despite what she'd told her earlier about him foaming at the corners of his mouth, Shayla threw Lennie a silent request to be her wingwoman. She practically snatched the glass from the friend and strutted away. Shayla kept a straight face. Christopher placed his hand on the small of her back to guide her. She couldn't help it. Something compelled her to take a quick look behind them. Her heart dropped. It caught her off guard to see Jamin looking directly at her.

CHAPTER 9

The group played two additional songs before ending the live performance to enjoy the remainder of the celebration. Jamin tried his best not to be obvious, but when Jace said he was going to find Lennie. He was low-key happy to tag along and decided to tell his friend about the guy he saw in her face.

"Aye uhh, Jace. I know you said y'all ain't a couple, but I don't want you to walk up on nothing. There was this guy up in her face when we were doing our set."

"Man, I ain't worried about no other nigga when I'm around." Jace shrugged.

"A'ight. I didn't know you had it like that."

"She just knows what's up."

They walked back to the other side of the mini-mansion, where some of the guests were lounging in a seating area with plush couches, accent chairs, and tables. Jamin nodded in the direction of Shayla, Lennie, and the guys. "There they are."

Jace took a step back and made sure they were out of their line of sight. "Now I ain't gon' front. She's grade-A. Nothing like I've ever had before. You wanna call her cousin Ms. Sunshine? Nah nigga, that right there, she got me ready to cut er'body off."

Jamin's eyebrows shot up. "She got you ready to do what now?"

"Sike, nigga! You know I'm playing." Jace laughed, delivering a playful punch to his chest.

"Aye, I wouldn't blame you though, if you did shut it down. 'Cause damn, Lennie fine as hell." Jamin said, admiringly.

He shifted his gaze to where Lennie sat. Jace quickly pulled his phone from his pocket. Jamin observed as his friend keyed in a message and leaned against the wall. A couple of minutes passed. Then Lennie checked her phone. She almost tripped over her own feet when she got up. Jace glanced at him with a devilish grin.

"What did you say to her?"

Jace didn't respond. Instead, he walked away with a finger, gesturing for him to 'wait a minute.' While he waited, Jamin's attention went back to where his interest was—Shayla. She grinned, exposing the dimple in her left cheek. Her smile was infectious. She seemed to be enjoying the company of that guy, who happened to be in her face, laughing a little too hard. He was probably doing the most to impress her. *Did he just make her blush?* He was decent-looking, but he wasn't all that. Nothing Jamin needed to be concerned about. There was no competition. *Hold up! Why am I comparing myself to this nigga?* Jamin shook his head. He was acting like a creep while spying on Shayla with someone else.

"There you are. I've been looking for you." A woman's soft voice interrupted him from his peeping Tom activities.

Jamin looked down to see Kelly smiling up at him with a full-toothed grin. She brushed her fingers along his forearm and parted her full lips. She moistened them with her tongue and bit into the bottom one. Kelly inched closer and pressed her breasts against him. The red, strapless, bodycon dress clung to her curves like a glove. Jamin had to give it to Kelly. She was a beautiful woman with a brickhouse figure. His dick began to swell, letting him know he agreed. He reached down, adjusting himself, and let out a rugged whisper, "Damn girl."

"What? See something you like, Jamin?" she purred, batting her lashes at him.

He took a step back and cleared his throat. "Kels, what you want?"

"You, what else? But I'm going to have another drink with my girls. Make sure you let me know when you're leaving." She blew a kiss and sashayed away.

His eyes were still on her ass when Jace came up beside him. "Yooo, was that your girl Kels thick ass just now?"

He delivered an elbow to Jace's side. "How many times have I told you? She ain't my girl."

"Ow! Well, Ion see why not. Talking about me. As long as y'all been fucking off and on. She ought to be."

"You know damn well why that ain't never gonna happen. Anyway, what's up? Where did you dip off to?" Jamin saw Lennie had returned to Shayla, but she wasn't sitting down. She had Shayla off to the side, speaking in private.

"I went to see who Lennie was gonna chill with tonight. We 'bout to head out."

"So, you cock blocked the next nigga?"

"Nah, she knows *this* dick. Why try something new that might be whack?"

Jamin laughed, shaking his head. "And I guess she's leaving her cousin stranded with them niggas?"

"She said she was gonna let her know we was out. And shit, Shayla might get down like Lennie does."

Doing his best not to sound too concerned, Jamin probed. "Whatchu mean get down like Lennie does?"

"See, y'all wanna be funny 'bout us making this official, but we do this with no strings attached. We have an understanding, and she's good with it. Ion know, but maybe Shayla fucks with that dude. Maybe not. If she does, it's probably with no strings attached. Ain't none of us got time for that anyway." Jace smelled his fingers. "Ahh yes, now, if you will excuse me, I got some grade-A pussy that's been marinating all night that I need to tenderize. I'll see you on Monday, my damie."

He watched his best friend walk over to where the cousins were. Giving zero fucks, Jace held out a hand. Lennie grabbed it and walked out with him without so much as a glance back at the guy she'd been chatting with for the last hour. Shayla tried to smooth it over with the guy she left behind, giving him a sympathetic smile. She got up to follow Lennie and Jace, and so did the other guy who'd been in her face. His hand went to the small of Shayla's back. Jamin clenched his jaw. He had to look away. He needed to pull himself together. It shouldn't've mattered, but it bothered him they were leaving together.

Was Shayla going to sleep with that guy?

That question plagued his thoughts more than half an hour later when he was on the way home. It continued to pop up at the forefront of his mind after he decided to let Kelly come through. He figured if he was balls deep in the pussy of the beautiful vixen, it would keep his psyche off Shayla Starr.

If what Jace said about her cousin is true … then is Shayla? No! He didn't want to think about what she might be doing with that guy right now.

"Mmhmm—gawk, gawk. Jamin mmhmm—gawk, gawk … *Pop!* Oooh so good mmhmm—gawk, gawk."

Jamin peered down at Kelly, licking, sucking, and choking on his dick. For a brief second, her face morphed into Shayla's. *What the fuck? Why is this girl still invading my thoughts?* Shaking his head, Jamin eased out of Kelly's mouth. Spittle dribbled down her chin and in between her breasts. She'd given his dick a wet, slick Armor All shine. Would Shayla be able to deep-throat his dick like this too? His thoughts began to wander as he saw her glossed lips instead. Jamin held Kelly by the throat and shoved his dick back inside to the hilt. He pumped his hips in and out. Tears rolled over his thumbs as he stuffed Kelly's mouth. He tried to push past her tonsils. She pressed her hands against his thighs, forcing him to take a step back. When he pulled out, she gagged and gasped for air.

"Dammit, Jamin! I almost threw up!"

He didn't respond. Instead, he went over to the side of the bed, took a condom from the nightstand, and wrapped up. Scooting to the middle of the California king bed, he leaned back and stared at Kelly, who remained on the floor, trying to gather herself. To keep the erection, he tugged on his shaft. She cut her eyes at him, but without another complaint, she pushed herself up from the floor and began a seductive walk over to the bed.

She climbed on and did a slow crawl up to him. Hovering over, Kelly planted her feet on either side of Jamin's thighs. Replacing his hand for hers, she took a firm grip on his shaft. Aligning her pussy above his tip, she kept her eyes on him and lowered herself onto his dick, gobbling every inch. She moved her hands, placing them firmly on his shoulders, and began rotating her hips.

Jamin grunted when her pussy clamped down on his shaft. She released him long enough to raise her ass up. The sound of her cheeks smacking against his thighs echoed off the walls when she dropped down. He jerked his head back when he felt the squeezing around his dick. Kelly repeated the Kegel exercises and see-sawing movement, riding him hard until she got the first orgasm out of the way. She kept going chasing after another one. Jamin laid back while she worked her hips up, down, and twirled around his dick. He didn't help. He didn't have to. This was Kelly's show. It always was. Suddenly, his thoughts shifted back to Shayla. He wondered if she took control like this. *Would she take what she wanted? Or was she a pillow princess?*

"Ohmygod Jamin, slap my ass! Please!"

Yanking him out of his thoughts about Shayla, Jamin did as Kelly commanded and delivered a hard one to her right cheek. Her pussy tightened around his shaft. Without needing additional instructions, he followed up by giving her left cheek the same attention. Again, her silky walls clutched his shaft tight. He gave her another, then another, followed by another, and another. Her walls constricted with each slap he gave. Kelly increased the speed of her gyrating.

"Yes! Yes! That's it! I'm about to ... I'm about to—ooooh!"

Kelly screamed at the top of her lungs, bucking until she collapsed next to him. She threw a limp arm across his chest, but Jamin didn't cuddle with her. That wasn't something they did. Once her labored breathing subsided, Kelly got up and sauntered into his master bathroom. By the time she came back with the warm washcloth, Jamin had already discarded the empty condom in the wastebasket next to the bed. He hadn't nutted and took a mental note she didn't bother checking if he did. She focused on cleaning him thoroughly before returning to the bathroom to take care of her hygiene. She'd gotten ready to lie down beside him when her phone rang.

"Hello ... He didn't? But he said he was ... Mama I know, but. Yes, I'll be there in about forty-five minutes. Okay, bye."

She ended the call and turned toward him. "Jamin, baby, I'm sorr—"

He held up a hand as he sat up. Rising from the bed, Jamin went to the armoire on the other side of the room. There were no words while she dressed. He threw on a pair of basketball shorts and slipped his feet into the Nike slides by the door. After putting her sandals on and grabbing her 'spend the night bag,' Kelly followed him out of the room and down the stairs. He almost laughed out loud, hearing *Let Me Go* by Daniel Caesar filtering through the speakers in the foyer. It amplified the sound of their mutual silence. He had nothing to say. Jamin reached for the doorknob.

Kelly came up on her toes. She planted a kiss on his cheek. "Okay, baby, I'll see you next time."

Without making eye contact, Jamin droned out, "Bye, Kels."

While keying in the code to the alarm system, he watched her back out of the driveway. He didn't know why he continued this endless cycle with her. Almost three years, and they were going nowhere. The nerve of Jace to say she ought to be his girl. *Who was he kidding?* Kelly could never be his girl. She belonged to the streets.

Heading back upstairs, Jamin thought back to how it was when they first met. They'd been on tour. Kelly was one of the backup singers to a different artist who was added to the tour lineup during the last leg. There wasn't any denial of his immediate physical attraction to her. He'd never been into skinny girls, and Kelly was far from it. She had the slim-thick shape, luscious Hollywood lips, and a perfect white smile. He could spend all day gazing into her dark brown eyes, which had an upward slant. When she laughed, they closed tighter, and he'd tease her about it. Once they came off tour, the pair were inseparable. They spent a lot of time together in the studio while he and his band worked on recording their second album. She'd even helped with some of the background vocals. Jamin realized their relationship had been anchored by the music. He couldn't think of anything else they had in common other than music and good sex. His cousin Cami warned him Kelly was looking for a come-up, but he'd been so gone over her he never saw the betrayal coming.

While they were out on tour again, word got back to him she'd been seen getting chummy with one of his label mates, Saint Luc. When he returned home and confronted her, Kelly denied there was anything going on between them. Things escalated during a BlakBeatz's party when Saint Luc taunted him about sleeping with Kelly. She'd claimed that Saint Luc was lying, and he meant nothing to her. The two men ended up fighting, with Jamin knocking Saint Luc out. The next month, Kelly revealed she was pregnant. Jamin knew it couldn't have been his baby. They'd never had sex without protection. Seven months later, while on tour, he found out from a post on Instagram the baby was Saint Luc's.

Jamin snatched the sheets from his bed and threw it in the hall. The cleaning service would be there in the morning. He relaxed on the fresh linen after a hot shower to cleanse his body and clear his mind. Folding his hands behind his head, he stared at the ceiling. Regardless of how good it might've felt, that needed to be the last time with Kelly. Once again, he used the head below instead of the one on his shoulders. Thinking of everything she'd put him through, Carl Thomas' song hit home hard. Jamin closed his eyes, wishing he'd never met Kelly.

CHAPTER 10

Shayla was halfway into her commute to Blakbeatz Studio and jamming to *Dreamlover*. The love ballad had been on repeat for most of the ride. Like her favorite singer crooned, she was also searching for a dream lover to rescue her with a love that would endure forever. A FaceTime call from Lennie interrupted her as she was in the middle of hitting a high note. She accepted, and her cousin's face appeared on the screen. Without fail, she unloaded a barrage of questions at Shayla.

"You didn't call. Does that mean the pretty boy had you bent over last night? How was it? Is he working with an anaconda or a Vienna sausage?"

Shayla groaned. "Umm, good morning to you too, Lennie, and no. Christopher did not have me bent over. Brunch at Nico's turned into an early dinner with unlimited drinks. I passed out when I got home. I'm glad I don't have a hangover."

"Hold up. I've been trying for months. How did y'all get in there?"

"A couple of his frat brothers own it. He made a call. We were in there for at least four, maybe five hours, just talking. I'll give him points there. He knows how to hold a conversation. Great sense of humor, and unlike those other dates I've had from hell, he didn't try to come back to my house after getting me drunk. But he put those soft lips on the back of my hand again, and I let him give me a quick peck."

"I wonder how long he can keep this up."

"What do you mean? Keep what up? What kinda vibe are you getting?"

"None, but this screams nice guy act. Look at what he's doing: dinner at upscale restaurants, the perfect gentleman doing random acts of kindness and teasing. You know, not forcing kisses. His goal is for you to throw the pussy at him. Trust me, he's ready to smash that bangin' body you got. I saw how he was looking at your ass."

Shayla sighed. "You're probably right. Even though I don't get a vibe that it's all about wanting to smash, it feels good that he's taking the time to date me. I just didn't realize he was that tall. I mean, he's not as tall as Jamin, but he's a nice height."

Lennie frowned. "Why are you comparing him to Jamin?"

"I-I'm not. Umm, I was just pointing out their height differences, that's all."

"Yeah, uh huh. Well, it's funny that you brought him up. I peeped that lil' exchange y'all two had at the piano on Saturday."

"I don't know what you're talking about." Shayla could hear her own nervous laugh.

"Girl, please, you can act like it was nothing, but I know what I saw. Jamin was singing to you, and your ass was caught up in all his fineness. You jumped when I tapped your shoulder to let you know Christopher was there."

"Whatever. I wasn't caught up in anything. It's a beautiful song. The lyrics had me, not him. Anyway, Christopher wanted to listen in while we record, so he's coming to the studio today. We're going to dinner afterward."

"Ooh, Jace asked me to swing by. So, I'll be there too."

It was Shayla's turn to tease her cousin. "Uh huh, for somebody that's just friends, you and Jace sure do act like it's more. Don't pretend he didn't cut in on Christopher's friend trying to holler at you."

She saw Lennie smirk with a flippant shrug of the shoulder. "He simply reminded me that whatever his name is, was unknown territory. Why would I want to sample something that might be worthless when I could get some of what I know will be amazing? I needed no further convincing. Look at this glow. Don't I look amazingly well fucked?"

"Yes, your forehead is rather shiny this morning."

"Fuck you."

She laughed, but relief settled in. Lennie hadn't pressed for more on her remark about Jamin. Since Saturday, Shayla had been subconsciously drawing contrasts between Jamin and Christopher. She wasn't sure exactly when or how it happened, but she was unable to deny it did. Unexpectedly, she caught feelings for the sexy grouch. Deep down, she knew it was mutual. The words he sang to her the other night seemed to be heartfelt. That was impossible. He had a girlfriend. She considered Christopher as the better option. Unlike Jamin, he was available. He had a job as a software engineer. He claimed to have no baby mamas, great credit, and investments. What did she have to lose? Her issue with Christopher was there weren't any sparks like she felt with Jamin.

Lennie's voice cut through her mental debate. "I'm glad to hear that you had fun with Christopher. Who knows, pretty boy might be around for a while."

"We'll see. All right, I just pulled up at the studio."

"Perfect timing. I gotta go get ready. See ya later."

After singing their usual goodbye, Shayla ended the call. A few minutes later, she entered the live room to find Daria and Zayne setting up. "Good morning!" She sang as she strolled over to the cabinet to put her bookbag away.

Daria waved. "Hey girl, hey!"

"What's up, newbie?" Zayne greeted with an upward head nod.

Shayla set her cup on the stand and grabbed the microphone. "I'm ready to sang. Y'all feel like warming up to another one of my faves? Who knows about love in A minor?"

"Say less, girly. Let's do this." Daria strummed a note on her guitar and leaned back in a power stance.

Shayla stood in front of the piano. "Do you think he'd mind?"

"Mind what?" Jace's voice startled her.

She quickly stepped away.

He chuckled. "What you know about ticklin' them ivories, girl?"

"I know a lot, but I don't want no problems with Oscar." Shayla waved her hands in front of her.

They all laughed. Jace gestured toward the bench. "He ain't here, newbie." He looked down at his watch. "And I doubt he'll be here anytime soon. What was y'all 'bout to do?"

"I wanted to warm up to a lil' love in A minor. You good with that?"

Jace spoke over his shoulder as he made his way to the drums. "Lemme see ya work, newbie."

She cracked her knuckles, then angled her head in his direction to wait for the signal to begin. Jace gave a slight head bob. Shayla belted out the acapella opening of Alicia Keys' *Fallin'*. Her fingers glided across the keys, playing the familiar melody. When she finished, they praised her for having another talent. They didn't know she could play the piano. They continued their jam session with Shayla joining Daria and Zayne on another hit: Maroon 5's, *She Will Be Loved*.

Shayla convinced her bandmates to recreate a scene from the rock band, Extreme's video. She sat across from Zayne while he played his guitar. Jace and Daria were seated in front of them. They used the lights from their phones as if they were lighters. Jamin walked into the room right while she crooned out the lyrics to *More Than Words*. He must've woken up on the wrong side of the bed that morning. Not only was he later than usual, Oscar the grouch also seemed irritated.

He sat down at the bench and snarled. "This is what y'all in here wasting time doing instead of practicing?"

Jace jumped up. "Aye man, we been waiting for you to get started."

"You ain't gotta wait for me to practice your parts. I'm here now. We got work to do, and y'all have wasted enough time. Let's get to it."

Shayla and Zayne followed Daria's example and sprang from the couch. Shayla quickly put her chair back in the corner and returned to the microphone. The lighthearted mood moments earlier turned sour. She lowered her head and focused on the sheet music in front of her. Even though she could sense Jamin's eyes burning a hole through her, she avoided looking up. Throughout the remainder of the morning, his patience continued to be short with everyone. The poor runner got it the worst. She'd gotten his lunch order incorrect. Not once, but twice. Jamin's outburst of anger caused her to bolt from the room in tears. Shayla wouldn't have blamed the girl if she quit after being reprimanded like that. Zayne pulled him to the side and tried reasoning with him to apologize, but Jamin wasn't hearing it. He yanked away in a huff.

"Why are you defending incompetence? She should've been listening instead of scrolling TikTok."

Ursula entered the room with Jamin's correct order. She set the bag down but didn't leave. She stood over him with her hands on her hips. He remained quiet as the older woman chewed him out.

Jace egged her on, clapping. "Yeah, Ursula, you tell him! Coming in here acting like we the ones he slept with last night. Did Kels piss in your cereal this morning?"

Shayla had to cover her mouth to keep from laughing. The icy glare Jamin gave him made her shudder. She, along with Daria and Zayne, bounced curious glances between the friends. As Jamin pelted him with ice daggers, Jace's brows shot up. There were unspoken words between them until Zayne cleared his throat. Jace threw his hands up. Without saying anything, he went to his drums and sat down.

Ursula continued scolding him. "I know a fight with Kelly's crazy tail wasn't that serious for you to go off on this girl and make her cry like that."

Jamin bit back, "I wish y'all would stop bringing her name up. It ain't Kels, damn! And twice Ursula, she got my lunch wrong. Twice! Anybody would've gotten pissed off. What they call it, hangry?"

She pursed her lips and folded her arms across her chest. "Boy, please."

"And you know we ain't got all day. I was trying to eat. Shit, she could've brought me a Snickers."

"The nerve of you. What time did you get in here?"

When he didn't respond, Ursula scoffed. "I swear you gon' make me cuss. Look here, I'm tired of you running all these people off now. This is getting old. I ain't got the time nor the patience to be training 'em. Cut this mess out and act like your mama 'nem raised you better."

"Ursula—"

"Jamin, don't play with me, boy. I know you better than you think." Ursula warned with a playful mush to his head and stormed out. When the door closed, Jamin turned his attention to Jace.

He pleaded with his friend, "I wish you would quit doing that shit, eggin' her ass on. Like I said, Kels ain't even the issue this time."

Jace's brows furrowed. "Well, if ain't Kels, then why you—"

"Just drop it. We're wasting time. And we need to get back to work. I wanted to run something by y'all anyway. I'mma eat while y'all check it out."

Jamin shared that he'd come up with another track. He handed out copies of the sheet music to everyone. While he ate, Shayla, along with the rest of the crew, practiced their parts. Shayla loved the lyrics. She had them ingrained in her memory by the time he finished eating. For the next couple of hours, they went through several runs of the new song.

They were discussing the final run-through of the day when one of the sound engineers knocked on the window. Everyone looked up. Shayla saw her cousin Lennie waving. She was about to wave back, but noticed Lennie's eyes weren't on her. It was Jace who had her cousin's attention. He teased Shayla with a big grin. Gesturing to the window, he signaled for Lennie to come into the studio with them.

"I think you and my cousin are too cute."

"Yeah, Lennie's my peoples." Jace beamed.

She was about to tease Jace, but the door to the studio opened. More than Lennie's voice filtered in. Shayla recognized who the other voice belonged to right as he came into view. Christopher strutted in, and right away, his eyes found hers. She gave a polite wave. He returned the wave and followed Lennie over to the seating area. There were two plush couches set up in the center to watch the band practice. Shayla should've felt excited to have him there. However, an uneasiness settled over her. Something in the room shifted. There was a palpable sense of tension. She stole a glance at Jamin. He didn't hide the eye roll from her as his jaw clenched tight. He pushed the bench out, got up from the piano, and went to Jace. Jamin faced him, giving his back to Christopher and Lennie.

His voice was a low growl as he leaned in. "What the fuck is he doing here?"

It wasn't low enough. Shayla walked over to them. The scent of Jamin's cologne punched her right in the nose. For a brief second, she was thrown off. Her eyes went to his broad chest. She could get a good look at it from her height. There were well-defined pecs hiding underneath his white tee. Instead of the group's logo, he rocked a designer tee, which accentuated his muscular upper body. The endless tattoos caught her attention. Shayla's lips parted.

Jamin frowned. "What?"

His voice snapped her out of the daze. Shayla straightened her back. She refused to let her voice lack confidence. Bringing her eyes up to meet his, she announced. "I invited him. Is there a problem?"

"Yeah. I wanted these sessions closed 'cause this is new music. Ain't nobody 'pose to be back here." He twisted his head, shooting Jace a menacing glare.

"What? Lennie's been back here before when we recorded new tracks. Shit, she's part of BlakBeatz."

Jamin cut his eyes back to Shayla. "He shouldn't be here."

"Well, too late. He's here now. It would be hella rude to tell him to leave with my cousin sitting there. I'll just make sure it won't happen again."

Not giving Jamin a chance to argue with her, Shayla walked away. She took her place in front of the microphone and closed her eyes. She silently counted backward from ten to one. She inhaled deeply and exhaled slowly. When she opened her eyes, Christopher's were directly on hers. He winked. Shayla cringed when she heard Jamin grumble.

"Since folks wanna eye fuck, let's get this last run done so we can get outta here."

Rather than letting his snarky comment get to her, she concentrated on centering herself and giving it her all. She wasn't about to give the grouch a reason to embarrass her in front of a guest. Five minutes later, Shayla thanked the musical gods for hearing her prayers. She opened her eyes to the guys behind the window, holding their thumbs up. There was nothing Jamin could complain about. They nailed it.

"Hells yeah!" Jace cheered.

Lennie came over to her, clapping. "Go off then! That shit was fire! I can't wait for them to put that one in rotation. I'm gonna have it on replay. Shay, you sound so good!"

"Yes, Shayla. Your voice is as beautiful as you are." Christopher smoothly co-signed.

Jamin smacked his teeth and croaked out a mirthless, bitter laugh.

Shayla stiffened. She was certain she heard him mumble, *This corny ass nigga.'* The embarrassed expression she gave Lennie was impossible to conceal. Lennie's eyes darted to Jace. He, in turn, looked to Daria. She turned her head to Zayne.

Zayne quickly bent down to pack up his guitar and other belongings. "Yep! Time to go!"

When Shayla's gaze locked on Jamin, he pinned her with a heated glare. She couldn't explain it, but there was a lot being said in his eyes.

Jace cleared his throat, breaking up the awkward silence. He grabbed Lennie's hand and headed towards the exit. "A'ight, y'all, we gon' head out. Catch up with y'all tomorrow night. I know Jazzmine's 'bout to be lit!"

Shayla finally tore her eyes away from Jamin. She quickly went over to the cabinet to grab her things. After mumbling good night, she gestured for Christopher to follow, and scurried from the room. She hadn't thought about where she was going until they were halfway across the parking lot, and Christopher tugged on her arm.

"Whoa, slow down for a second." He eased her back to him.

She spun around. "I'm sorry. I didn't even ask where you parked."

"Hey, you good? Listen, I heard how Jamin can be. Did I miss something back there?"

Shayla chewed the inside of her jaw. Jamin was upset, and she didn't want to think it had anything to do with her, yet she knew better. It was clear what was going on after he made the remark about Christopher being there, the two of them eye-fucking, and then his reaction to Christopher's compliment. *Is Jamin jealous? No. He couldn't be. He has a girlfriend.* Shayla thought to herself.

"Shayla?" Christopher's voice interrupted her internal musings.

She peeked up at him. "Uhh yeah, I'm good. And no, you didn't miss anything. Jamin's been like that all day. He was going through something and taking it out on everybody. He'll be fine. Anyway, we were going to dinner, right?"

"Yes, and I'm starving. I'll walk you to your ride."

Once she climbed into her SUV, Christopher gave her the name of the restaurant where to meet him. She pressed the ignition button. After hearing the engine purr to life, Shayla sat for a minute after he walked away. The nagging thought in the back of her mind about Jamin's actions prompted her to send Lennie a text. Out the corner of her eye, Shayla saw Jamin come out of the building. His head whipped in her direction. Their eyes connected. Unable to stop herself, Shayla pushed the button to let the window down. It was as if a magnet was drawing them closer to one another. Jamin started heading in her direction. He paused. His eyes briefly strayed from hers to focus on something else before returning to her. Like earlier, he held her with an intense gaze that said more than words. Sudden ringing startled her. Her breath hitched. Shayla leaned back, splaying a hand against her chest. She saw the name on the display of her dashboard. Pressing a button on the steering wheel, she stammered out, "H-hello?"

The SUV echoed with Christopher's deep voice. "I was heading out the parking lot, but I saw you were still sitting there. You good?"

She glanced out the window. Jamin was gone. She closed it and shifted into reverse. Shayla cleared her throat. "Uhh yeah. Yeah everything's fine. I was putting the directions in my phone. I'm backing out now. Meet you there in just a few."

Shayla ended the call. As she drove away, her gaze returned to the spot where Jamin had been. She shook her head, asserting she had to focus on her date with Christopher.

How am I supposed to do that with this grouch on my mind?

CHAPTER 11

Jamin realized Jace had been right when he said Jazzmine's Place would be lit. The line to get inside was already extended around the corner when they arrived earlier. The popular jazz lounge and dance club always kept a big crowd. However, with their live performance that night, the two-story establishment reached its maximum capacity. Jamin could see from the stage there was no seating available. As he read the posts and scrolled his Instagram feed, he saw the fans who couldn't get in begging for an encore performance. He and Jace were at the bar, low-key eavesdropping on the discussion Derrik and Jazzmine, the owner's wife, were having.

"Derrik, this has never happened. I felt so bad turning them away."

"I guess you have LMK to thank for shutting it down."

"Heh, you're welcome. It's what we do." Jace leaned over, bragging.

Jamin gave him a playful shove but beamed with pride. "I ain't gon' front Jazz. It feels good to know we caused that. But hey, if it's cool with D, and you have the opening on your calendar, we could squeeze in one more show before we head out to Vegas next month." He held up his phone. "The fans want it."

Derrik nodded in agreement. "I'm good with it so long as Jazz can make it happen."

She motioned towards the hall that led to the back. "Come. Let's go to my office and check. If the timing works, we can lock it in now. Then we need to get our marketing teams working on this A-S-A-P."

They were a few feet away when Jace turned to face him. He leaned in. "I'm surprised Kels ain't here. Where she at?"

"Probably couldn't get her mama to baby—" Jamin's brows knitted together. "Nigga, Ion know. And I done told you, she ain't my girl!"

"A'ight, now I know something's up. You always fuck with Kels. Matter of fact, you wanna tell me what the fuck is going on? What really was up with you yesterday if it wasn't Kels?"

Jamin was about to open his mouth, but the bartender approached the counter. He placed the order for them. While she poured double shots of whiskey, he avoided making eye contact with his best friend and massaged the back of his neck. He knew at some point Jace would want to address his behavior the day before. More than likely, he was also asking on behalf of Zayne and Daria. If it wasn't Jace, eventually, Zayne would've been the one asking questions. He'd had no intentions of telling any of them what he was feeling. He was going to let it go. He had to, for the obvious reasons. Shayla was into this guy, Christopher. At that exact moment, her laughter found its way to his ears.

Jamin peeked at Jace before glancing over his shoulder. He'd grown to love that sound as much as her angelic voice, but hated it was that guy making her laugh. He grumbled something inaudible. His jaw tightened. Picking up the shot glass, he threw it back. Jamin tapped the bar, signaling for the bartender.

"Ahhh, I get it now." Jace snorted and threw his shot back. He nodded at the bartender for another shot as well.

"You get what now?"

"You feeling Shayla."

Jamin leaned back and ran his fingertips around the rim of the glass. He didn't confirm nor deny his best friend's statement. He couldn't. As much as he wanted her, it was pointless.

"Don't matter now, do it?" Jamin gritted out, rising to his feet.

"Hey, where you going?"

He spoke over his shoulder. "To use the head."

Jamin kept his eyes straight ahead as he walked by the leather couches. He didn't look in the direction he'd heard Shayla's voice coming from. The group had gathered in the stylish VIP area after their performance to hang out there for the rest of the night. Shayla brought Christopher and a couple of his friends along. Even though Daria, Zayne, and Lennie joined them, Jamin opted to sit at the bar. He used the excuse he needed to speak with Derrik. There was no way he would sit around while Shayla flirted with another man. While in the restroom, Jamin thought about what he needed to do moving forward. He wasn't going to be pining over a woman who wasn't interested in him. He also knew he couldn't continue being rude to everyone out of frustration either. Without knowing exactly what he would do next, he tossed the paper towel in the trash can and exited the restroom. Jamin hit the corner but halted in his steps when he heard a couple of voices coming from the hallway.

"Aye man, what's up with Shayla? I still can't believe you got with her sexy ass."

"What you mean? You act like she could resist all of this swag. Ha!"

"Whatever nigga. Well, at least one of us ended up winning 'cause them cousins is bad as hell. I hate that fine-ass Lennie ain't trying to fuck on nobody 'cept that dread head drummer. If she gave a nigga half a chance that night, I woulda had her ass bent like a pretzel. So, what's up? You hit that yet?"

"Nah. I'mma handle that tonight."

"Wait. You mean to tell me you been wining and dining her ass for almost three weeks, and she ain't gave up the pussy yet? Man, if I took her to Capitol Grille, Nico's, and the Palms, her ass would've been slobbering on my wood by now. No, twerking that thick ass on it. Matter of fact, you need to bring her ass back here now so she can hit you off."

"Listen you idiot, a girl like Shayla ain't gonna put it out that fast. She's been through some shit. You know, damaged goods. Some dude hurt her bad. She ain't trusting no nigga just because he's taking her out for expensive food. So, I had to ease into this. Take it slower than usual. I ain't gotta wait no thirty days or nothing like that. But I had to pull out all the big words, tell her about my goals and aspirations. That shit. She just needs a lil' coaxing."

"You buggin'. Ain't no coaxing. Either she gon' put out or be out. Hold up. Ain't they going to Vegas next month? Nigga, she trying to hold out. She gon' make you wait thirty days and do all that prove you want me by doing this long-distance nonsense. Watch, you ain't getting shit."

"Look, I ain't worried. She's giving up the pussy tonight. I made sure to keep her ass on that Casamigos. A couple more shots, and she should be good. Come on, let me use this bathroom."

"Whoa man, watch it." Christopher's friend swerved to avoid a collision with Jamin's shoulder.

Without slowing his stride, Jamin snarled. "Nah, you watch it."

After eavesdropping on what Christopher and his friend said about Shayla and her cousin, Jamin saw red. He wanted to punch both men in the mouth as they passed him in the hallway. He had no intention of moving out of the way of the friend who did the most talking. In fact, he secretly wished the man would've run into his shoulder. Jamin was ready to give him a two-piece where it guaranteed he would see the stars. When he returned to the bar, Jace nodded at the shot waiting for him. Jamin didn't waste any time throwing it back. He raised his hand to get the bartender's attention and slumped down onto the stool. This time, he chose to face the lounge area where he could have a better view of Shayla. With them being a few feet away, it would also allow him to listen in on their conversation better. His face scrunched up as thoughts ran together on what he should do about what he'd heard. Then again, what could he do?

"Yo, I think you need to tell her if that's what you're feeling. If—"

Jamin held his hand up in a stop sign gesture. He twisted his head in Jace's direction. "Nah, she chose this dude. I wanna see how this shit plays out." Cocking his head to the side, he sent a silent signal to his friend. Jace bowed his head. Jamin rotated his head to look at Shayla again.

Whatever Lennie was describing, Shayla was totally absorbed in it. Then she threw her head back, laughing. Jamin's chest tightened. Every time that pit formed in her left cheek, it had an instant effect on him. The overhead strobe lighting made it appear as though she was under a spotlight. He'd seen what she wore, but he took a moment to appreciate the fun size vixen who had him smitten. Jamin's gaze traveled the length of her short, curvy frame from head to toe. Her faux locs were in an updo hairstyle, leaving her delectable, slender neck exposed. Her bare, caramel-colored shoulders shimmered under the light. The black, skintight dress stopped mid-thigh. With red bottom heels elevating her a couple of inches, the back of her calves looked more toned. Jamin moistened his lips as his gaze moved up to her round ass and slim waist. He finally fixed his gaze on her face, studying every feature. When he got to her mouth, it was partially open. Like always, those pouty lips shined from the gloss she wore. He lifted his eyes. She was staring right at him.

Shit!

He quickly shifted his focus from her to the wall-mounted televisions. Just then, Christopher and his friend returned. A bottle service girl followed with a round of shots, as Christopher planned. He and Shayla made a toast. Then Christopher leaned in, planting a kiss on her cheek. He lowered his head to whisper in her ear. Jamin groaned when Shayla's cheeks flushed, and she pressed her body closer to Christopher.

"You good?" Jace asked.

Staring intently at Christopher, Jamin narrowed his eyes. While he wasn't sure when he would have to intervene, watching that asshole touch her was frustrating. "Yeah, just hoping I won't have to break somebody's fingers tonight."

Jamin tipped his head in the direction of the lounge area. For the next half an hour, he kept a watchful eye as Shayla danced and had a few more shots. She appeared to be holding her own. Still, Jamin wasn't trusting Christopher not to try and take advantage of her. She'd just sat down when Lennie began making her way over to them. At the same time, Derrik and Jazzmine returned to confirm that LMK was on for another show the following weekend. While Jace and Lennie spoke to them about the logistics of the show, Jamin swung his attention back to Shayla. Without Lennie over there, his attentiveness kicked into overdrive.

"Jamin?"

He snapped his head in Derrik's direction. "What?"

"I asked if that's cool with you."

Being distracted by Shayla prevented him from hearing anything. Jamin and Jace exchanged a covert gesture, indicating Jamin needed assistance. His best friend responded with a slight nod of the head. Jamin rubbed his hands together. "Yeah, D, it's cool with me. Let's do this."

Jamin noted Derrik's facial expressions as he eyed him and Jace. Derrik walked over and stood next to him. He leaned in. His voice was low where only Jamin could hear. "You must think I'm fucking dumb. You didn't hear shit I said.

But I know that look, Jay. Is this going to end up a night like Saint Luc? I hope not, 'cause you not about to fuck up those money-making hands or Jazz's spot."

Jamin looked over his shoulder to meet Derrik's intense gaze. "Nah, D, it ain't gonna be like that. I won't let it get that far."

"Can I ask you something? Is it about Shayla?"

The two men stared at each other for a brief minute. Jamin tried to reassure him. "You have my word, D. I'm good. Nothing's gonna happen."

"How about Hodges will make sure of it?" Derrik gripped Jamin's shoulder, giving it a firm squeeze. "Look Jay, I get it. If anybody understands, it's me. Still, you need to keep your head, a'ight." He then repeated what Jamin missed and went back to say good night to Jazzmine.

Before he left, Jamin saw Derrik speaking to his bodyguard, who kept his eyes trained on him. There was no doubt in Jamin's mind Derrik told Hodges to make sure he didn't end up whooping somebody's ass. If Christopher didn't try anything with Shayla, there wouldn't be any problems. When he spotted Christopher guiding Shayla to the exit, he realized it was going to be something popping off.

Jamin quickly rose to his feet with his hands balled up at his sides.

"Aye, what's wrong with you?" Jace perked up.

Tilting his head, Jamin gestured in the Shayla's direction. "It's sorry niggas like him who give real men like me a bad rap. You had to hear his punk ass. Listening to that conversation made my stomach turn. It might not be my place, but I know one thing for sure. Shayla won't be leaving with his bitch ass."

"Who?" Jace questioned him, but he didn't respond.

Instead, he began heading toward the exit after them. Jamin heard a groan come from Hodges, and Lennie say, 'Oh shit.' He didn't stop until he was in the hallway that also led to the bathrooms. He was a few feet away from Shayla and Christopher. Two of Christopher's friends stood in between them. Jamin gave a smug smile when they turned around and looked up at him, Hodges, and Jace. They backed away with their hands up and moved to the side. Christopher had his back to them. He was too busy in Shayla's face to notice what was going on behind him.

His friend threw out a caution, "Chris, umm, why don't you let Shayla go?"

Jamin brought his arms across his chest. He cut his eyes at the guy. It was the same friend from earlier that'd suggested the opposite. Christopher wrapped an arm around her waist. It was then Jamin noticed Shayla's balance was off.

"Nah, 'cause baby girl said she was ready to go, right?"

She whined. "No, Christopher, I said I had to go to the bathroom."

"Well, I'm ready to go and get you outta this." He ran a hand up her thigh.

Shayla grabbed his wrist. "Stop. What are you doing?"

"I'm gonna give you a night you won't forget, Shayla Starrrrr." Christopher growled and nuzzled into her neck.

Shayla pleaded, "No."

"No, what, baby?"

"This isn't what I want."

"Then what you want, baby?" Christopher pressed his body against hers. "'Cause you know I can give it to you."

Christopher's hand cupped her breast. Shayla slapped his hand away. "No! Stop it!"

His friend tried to reason with him. "Aye yo, Chris, just let her go, man."

Jamin gritted his teeth and moved in right as Shayla glanced over Christopher's shoulder. Her eyes bulged when they met his.

She pushed against Christopher's chest. "Get off of me!" Her shove was hard enough to loosen his grasp on her. She stumbled backward, but managed to keep her balance.

Christopher took a step toward her. Shayla shook her head back and forth with a hand extended in front of her. "No!"

"No? What you mean?"

Shayla spat. "It's a complete sentence."

"It sure is, asshole," Jamin affirmed with a chuckle.

Christopher whirled around, shock registering in his expression. His eyes widened for a second, then his eyebrows slammed together. He glanced back at Shayla, pointing his thumb at Jamin. "What's this about? You fucking him or something?"

"Best believe if she were, you wouldn't be standing there with her." Inching closer to him, Jamin puffed out his chest.

Christopher threw him a dismissive wave as he chortled. "Nigga, since you not, why don't you mind your fucking business."

He and Christopher exchanged scathing glares. Both refused to concede until Shayla's voice got his attention. "Jamin, please, I've got this."

"Nah, because from what I just saw and the shit I heard him and his boy saying earlier, you don't." Jamin's earnest stare shifted from his friend leaning against the wall back to Christopher. He looked Christopher from head-to-toe before mocking: "*She's damaged goods. Some dude hurt her bad. She ain't trusting no nigga just because he's taking her out for expensive food. So, you had to ease into this. Take it slower than usual. You ain't gotta wait no thirty days or nothing like that. But you had to pull out all the big words. Tell her about your goals and aspirations. That kinda shit. She just needs a lil' coaxing, right? But you ain't worried 'cause she's giving up the pussy tonight. You made sure to keep her ass on that Casamigos. A couple more shots, and she should be good, right?*"

Jamin turned to look at Lennie and then Jace. "And he's pissed Lennie decided to be fucking on you, the dread head drummer. But if she didn't, he said she would've been bent like a pretzel. These niggas been plotting on the cousins."

The color drained from Christopher's and his friend's faces.

Lennie blurted out, "What? You think I'd fuck you with that excess slob you got foaming at the mouth? You whack ass nigga!"

"Did you ... did you say those things about me?" Shayla choked out.

Christopher reached out for her.

Shayla yanked away. "No, is that what you think of me?"

"I mean, well, umm you know, it's just ... look, can I just talk to you away from all this?" Christopher gestured behind them.

Shayla sniffled. "No. I think it's better you just leave. I don't have anything to say."

Jamin saw the tears pooling in Shayla's ducts. She'd wrapped her arms around her body before starting to massage them. He wanted to pull her into his arms, but he needed to get rid of the trash. Throwing up his thumb, Jamin gestured for the exit. "You heard what she said. It's time for you to go, playa."

Next thing Jamin knew, Christopher turned and threw a punch. He ducked. Coming up swift, he connected with a right hook and an uppercut, sending Christopher's body sailing to the other side of the hall. He hit the floor with a loud thud. His friends ran over to him. He was out cold. Hodges quickly walked over, giving them instructions to get Christopher's inebriated ass up and out of there. He also advised them to let Christopher know there was no confrontation. The way everybody else saw it, he'd fallen and hit his face on the way out. His friends nodded in agreement before hoisting Christopher up and leaving out the back door.

"Yooooo, I can't believe you hit homie with a two-piece, Jay!" Jace cheered.

Jamin shook his head. He couldn't celebrate with his best friend. Not yet. Jamin's eyes never left Shayla. Lennie was talking to her, but Shayla looked where Christopher was laying. She didn't respond. He wanted to be the one to wipe away the tears streaming down her cheeks. Finally, he tapped Lennie on the shoulder. "May I?"

Jace grabbed Lennie's hand. "Come on, my boy's got her."

Jamin gave Lennie a reassuring nod and waited for them to leave. He reached out for Shayla, but she swatted at his hand and jerked away.

"No! Don't act like you care!"

Jamin pleaded, "Come on, don't be like that. I do."

She smacked her teeth and folded her arms across her chest. He reached out for her again but let his hand drop to his side. "Okay, I can be a grouch sometimes, but it don't mean I don't care."

"You didn't have to help me." Shayla sniffled, wiping her face with the back of her hand.

"But I did because I care. Did you not hear me? Look, we not about to beef about this."

Her eyebrows shot up. "*We*? There is no we! You already have a girlfriend!"

"No, I ... Shayla, wait a second! If you let me—"

"Ugh, just leave me alone!" She cried while storming off to the restroom.

Jamin pinched the bridge of his nose. "Fuck!"

"Ahem, Jamin?"

It was Hodges and another guy from his team. Jamin knew they needed to know what the next steps were. He shot them an upward head nod. "Hey Hodg, thanks for taking care of his friends. I know D won't like knowing I lost my head for a minute." He held up his hands. "No worries though. I'm good. Didn't break anything this time. Nothing a pain reliever and a lil' soak in ice overnight won't take care of. I know you see there are a few cameras. Could y'all get with Jazz to take care of any footage? Oh, and can you make sure Shayla gets home?"

Hodges nodded. The men exchanged daps before leaving him. Jamin glanced back at the women's restroom. He started walking, but headed for the exit. Shayla wanted space. He'd give her that, for now.

CHAPTER 12

Shayla cut her eyes from Lennie and focused on her reflection in the mirror as she brushed her hair down from the wrap. She worked her fingers through her hair, which still held its curls. Picking up the tube of Fenty Gloss Bomb, she puckered up and applied a layer of the shimmering pearl color to her full lips.

"I think you're overreacting."

She glanced down at her phone. "You would think that because it wasn't you on the receiving end of that debacle last night."

"You can't be serious right now, Shay. If anything, Jamin did you and me a favor. Christopher was an asshole. Remember, I said his pretty ass was probably putting on a nice guy act. I was hoping he wasn't playing you. Looks like he was doing all that just to get some ass. Dummy should've said that from the door." Lennie chided.

Shayla got up from her vanity. Picking up her phone, she left the master bathroom and went into her bedroom. She plopped down on the bed, whining to Lennie as she complained. "See what I mean. Ugh! Chalk this up as another one of the most embarrassing moments in my adult life, okay? The sexiest man on earth had to come to my rescue because a pretty boy, the one that you said was putting on the nice guy act to get my cookies, was, in fact, putting on a nice guy act to get my cookies!"

"Shay Bae, did you just say—"

"And for the record, when he asked if I was ever hurt, I told him about that asshole Trevor because I thought we were sharing our pasts for a better understanding of who we were getting ready to date. So now I'm not trusting niggas. That sexy ass man had to hear that I'm damaged goods. Ugh all over again! Then I guess pretty boy thought taking me out for some expensive food was the move. But I didn't ask him to, Len! Hmph, he was the one who wanted to wine and dine me, taking it slow. Pssh, using all those big words to impress me. I didn't even understand what the fuck he was saying half the time with that engineer mumbo jumbo. And to be honest, I didn't give a fuck about his goals and aspirations! If it wasn't about music, I tuned his ass out. I should've known something was up last night. His whole vernacular switched up with his friends around, but I was too tipsy to figure it out."

When Shayla paused to take a breath, she noticed Lennie had a fist covering her mouth.

"What the hell did I just say that you found funny?" she squealed.

"Since when did Jamin become the sexiest man on earth?"

Shayla blinked a few times. "Wh-what are you talking about?"

"You called Jamin sexy not once, but twice in that little rant you just had."

"I did?"

"Don't play dumb, Shay."

She couldn't hide the scarlet hue staining her cheeks. Even her laugh came out sounding nervous. "I'm not."

"Uh huh, then admit it."

"Admit what?"

"That Jamin's the sexiest man on earth."

Shayla couldn't keep herself from blushing.

"Look at you! Your ass been crushing on that man. I think we already know how he feels about you. That song he sang to you at the party. And look at how he acted that day pretty boy was at the studio session. He wasn't feeling his ass then. What are you gonna do, cuzzo?"

"Absolutely nothing. Besides, he has a girlfriend. Kelly, or whatever her name is." Shayla rolled her eyes.

"Kelly Nichols? You mean Saint Luc's baby mama? The same Kelly that gets ran through by er'body. Hell, she puts Jace to shame from what I heard."

Shayla's eyes grew wide. "Are you for real? But I saw her with Jamin a week ago at Black Coffee. She was all in his face and called him baby."

"So, that don't mean nothing. Now, if my memory serves me right, some years ago, I believe they used to mess around. But nah, that ain't his girl. Kelly Nichols is for them streets."

"Well, I still have to work with him. And I don't want to complicate anything or make this weird. It's better to keep it professional. We ain't Ashford & Simpson."

Lennie laughed. "I can dig that. But the question is, how long he can keep it professional?"

Shayla shrugged.

"Well, what you got planned for the rest of the day? I see you getting all pretty."

"I'mma swing by the studio. Wanna get this track outta my head. Maybe the mall later."

"All right, hit me up. We can meet up and swing by Atlantic Station for drinks."

The cousins sang their goodbyes, and Shayla made her way to the studio. She was relieved to find none of her bandmates' vehicles, particularly Jamin's truck, were in the parking lot. Shayla entered the live room and dropped her bag on the floor next to the piano. She slid onto the bench. Thinking of how Jamin's fingers made beautiful melodies from the massive instrument brought a smile to her face.

"I've got one that's been sitting in the back of my head, Mr. Love."

Shayla blew out a breath and stretched her fingers. Gliding them across the keys, she played the familiar chords to *Whenever You Call*. However, she didn't sing the original lyrics. Instead, Shayla sang the words she'd written. She got to the chorus when she heard a male voice singing along from behind. Gasping, Shayla clutched her chest and hopped from the bench.

"Why'd you stop?"

"Uhh, you scared me."

"My bad. You sound amazing, like a … like an angel. Come on. Let's finish." Jamin outstretched his hand.

Shayla didn't miss the smirk on his face when he reached the bench and motioned for her to sit. The sexy grouch had the nerve to be wearing a short-sleeve, red polo, revealing those tatted muscular arms. The relaxed-fit jeans fit comfortably around his waist, and the designer sneakers completed the look of a model walking off the pages of a magazine. His locs were neatly tied into a bun. Her heart did a backflip and then a somersault. The beating wouldn't slow down. It was as though she'd ran a one-hundred-meter dash. As soon as he sat down, the intoxicating woodsy fragrance, along with his natural musk, filled her nostrils. Shayla held onto the bench to keep from swooning. She loved the way he smelled.

"I didn't know you could play the piano."

"My daddy taught me."

"Yeah, mine did too. A'ight, newbie, do your thang. And I'll do the other part."

"Okay."

Pushing aside her nervous jitters, Shayla's fingers found the keys to play. The moment Jamin sang the lyrics of Brian McKnight, her heart swelled. Both men could sing, but she preferred her sexy grouch's tenor sound. They continued through the song into the next stanza. The hairs on the back of Shayla's neck stood up. She sensed it before, but with him being next to her, there wasn't any denying it. Shayla knew where his eyes were. Twisting her head in his direction, she locked gazes with Jamin. The words resonated loud the moment she crooned them to him. She'd been inspired by him, and looking into his eyes, she found her soul. He had her heart wide open. Jamin became expressive with his hands in the next verse when it was his turn to sing again. Shayla could feel it. He meant every single word. They sang through the chorus to the outro, not once taking their eyes off one another. Their labored breathing was the only sound left in the room after the final note.

His light touch on her arm triggered several fireworks throughout her body. She looked down at the bumps forming on her bare arms. Her pussy twitched, leaking a lusty tale of what kind of effect he had on her. Shayla peeked up at Jamin, whose heated gaze was on her. He scooted closer until their faces were inches apart. Shayla's eyes were on his thick, pink lips. The bottom was plump and perfect for sucking. His tongue darted out, moistening them.

Her words came out in a breathless whisper. "Jamin, are you … are you about to-to kiss me?"

His voice was low and raspy, "Only if you want me to. Do you want me to kiss you, Shayla?"

Jamin tucked his bottom lip in his mouth and hooked a finger under her chin. Shayla was unable to stifle the moan that escaped her lips when he brushed his thumb across her bottom lip. Another puddle of lust flooded the seat of her panties. She squeezed her thighs tighter. Nodding, her voice was barely above a whisper. "Yes."

Slanting his head, Jamin slid his thumb away and replaced it with his soft, pillow-like lips. Shayla parted hers, and his peppermint-flavored tongue slipped inside. In the wet confines of her mouth, their tongues collided in a silent battle. She didn't put up a fight. His thick tongue conquered hers. She moaned, gripping his muscular biceps. Jamin's hands cradled the back of her neck, guiding her deeper into a dreamlike, erotic kiss. It was slow, passionate, and could have gone on forever. She felt the immediate void when he eased from her swollen lips, delivering lingering pecks until the moment finally ended.

Shayla's breasts heaved against him. "You, umm, kissed me."

He pressed his forehead against hers, growling against her lips. "I did. And I knew kissing you would be like this."

Shayla couldn't believe Jamin Love kissed her. She reached up to touch his full bottom lip. Her cheeks felt warm as a giggle slipped out. "Does this mean you-you like me?"

"I tried to deny it for so long, but I don't wanna anymore." Jamin lifted her up, placing her on his lap.

Shayla twisted her head to face him. Her mouth dropped open, and then she glanced down toward her lap. "Oh my god, Jamin. Is that … Jesus, you're … you're big!"

He nuzzled his face in her neck. "My sexy songbird, I doubt you'll have a problem handling it."

Another moan slipped out when Jamin trailed kisses down Shayla's neck. A lustful fire began to burn within her. He was right. Shayla's overwhelming desire for him gave her the confidence she could. Shayla snaked an arm around his neck. She pushed her ass firmly against his stiff erection.

Jamin raised his head. He took hold of her chin, guiding her to meet him at eye level. He pinned her with a direct gaze. Desire blazed in his eyes. Despite being low, his voice had an animalistic growl to it. "Shayla, I want you. Will you let me have you?"

Staring into his chestnut brown eyes, her pulse quickened. She knew she was powerless to resist his charm. There had been a mutual attraction ever since they met. A tingling sensation shot through her at the thought of her and Jamin making love. She felt her core clench and go slippery inside. Shayla removed his hands from her chin. Leaning closer, she teased his lips with a kiss and whispered, "Yes."

CHAPTER 13

Jamin came to a stop at the traffic light and peeked over at Shayla. He'd caught her shifting in the seat a few times. He'd even seen her pick imaginary lint balls from her pants. Though she could be chatty at times, he struggled to keep her engaged during the last ten minutes of their ride to his house. Her mind seemed to be somewhere else. He knew she was likely second-guessing her decision agreeing to come home with him and was a nervous wreck about it. He needed to help her relax. Jamin reached over, took hold of her small hand and brought it up to his lips, pressing a kiss on the back of it. Shayla's cheeks flushed. Jamin relished in knowing that it would be him from now on putting this look on her face. Out the corner of his eye, he saw the light turn green. His attention returned to the road, but he didn't let her hand go.

"Penny for your thoughts?"

She blew out a breath. "I'm thinking why now? What changed your mind because from day one, I could tell you didn't like me?"

Jamin nodded his head in agreement. "Yeah, as much I didn't like your ball of fire ass, you were a pleasant surprise. I ain't gonna front, I was more frustrated that I found myself attracted to you by the end of the day. Even when I tried my hardest not to, I still ended up thinking about you. And I'm talking 'bout more than just a little bit. I looked forward to seeing you, hearing your corny ass jokes, and that cute snort you do when you laugh hard."

"I do not snort, do I?"

"Yes, you do. But seeing you with that nigga had me feeling some type of way. That shit was fucking with me. I don't know how I was gonna deal with it if y'all ended up together. Nah, I wouldn't have. And the more I think about it, you wouldn't've anyway. I know you can't deny that there was something between us ... something that couldn't be ignored." He took his eyes off the road momentarily. "This thing between us needed to be explored." Before returning them to the road, his eyes searched hers.

Her voice was unsteady as the words came rushing out. "But this. Us. Are you sure, Jamin? Maybe this is a mistake. Like, are we really going to? No, should we? I mean, I want to. I do. I really do, but what does this mean? Is this going to be a one-time thing, or are we—"

"Shhh, you're thinking too much and worrying about the wrong stuff. But to answer your questions: This. Us. Yes, I'm very sure it's not a mistake. Yes, we're really going to do this. Yes, we should. It means that we both want each other. And hell no, this ain't gonna be no one-time thing." He glanced over at her briefly and winked before looking back in front of him. "You and me, oh, we're locked in from here on out. I plan on us doing this a lot and often."

Jamin stuck one of her fingers in his mouth and sucked it. Shayla relaxed against the headrest. She let out the sexiest-sounding moan. *Shit!* Knowing she would be calling his name, making that noise, and more, his dick gained a life of its own. His jeans were stretched tighter than ever with the pressure from his rapidly growing erection, causing it to ache. He released the finger and placed her hand back on her lap. Jamin reached down and adjusted himself. He needed to hurry up. Thankfully, after a right turn, his house was on the next street.

He pressed a button on the overhead panel to open the garage door. After parking, Jamin hopped out of his Cadillac Escalade. He rounded the truck in a haste to lift Shayla out. He made sure to slide her body along the front of his. She peered up at him with wide eyes.

"Come on." Jamin instructed with a cocky grin.

He guided her through a side door that led them into his massive kitchen. He lingered behind to bring up the sultry chill playlist on his phone. Jamin cued

Tonight by Black Atlass to play and looked up when Shayla turned around. The expression on her face read as if she were a kid in a candy store.

Her eyes went to the commercial-grade gas range as she squealed. "Jamin, this is a chef's dream kitchen. I've only seen one like it on HGTV. Do you cook in here? Wait, do you even know how to cook?"

He placed a hand on his chest. "Ouch! That cut me deep. Do you really think I got this custom-designed just for show? Yeah, I cook in here, and I know how to cook quite well. Thank you very much. Matter of fact, I'll make sure you get one of my signature dishes before you leave." Jamin moved closer and lowered his voice to a growl. "But right now, there's something else I'm hungry for and wanna eat."

Shayla clutched her chest and coughed.

"Thirsty? Need some water?"

She chortled, "Uh-huh, yes, please. Thank you."

Opening the Sub-Zero refrigerator with a chuckle, Jamin took out a couple of bottled waters. He unscrewed the cap on one and handed it to Shayla. After taking a swig from his bottle, he set it on the breakfast island. Tucking his bottom lip in his mouth, he watched as she gulped down almost half the bottle.

"Damn, girl. How is it you can make drinking bottled water so sexy?"

She almost choked. Quickly removing the bottle from her mouth, Shayla spilled some. Jamin caught her wrist before she could go for a paper towel. He rocked his head from side to side. Taking the bottle from her, he replaced the cap and set it on the island. He swooped in with his tongue to lick away the droplets of water from her chin and lip. Jamin's hand went to her lower back, and the other cradled the nape of her neck. Shayla's arms draped over his shoulders. Slanting his mouth over hers, he devoured her luscious mouth. He sucked, nibbled, and savored the sweet taste of the fruity candy that still lingered on her tongue from earlier. It was a brazen, earth-shattering kiss that set off a wild need in him.

Bending at the knees, Jamin cupped Shayla's ass and lifted her from the floor. He wrapped her legs around his waist. He retreated from their kiss long enough to instruct her to grab their waters. Once she had them, Shayla clasped her arms around his neck. He reconnected with her lips on his way out of the kitchen. Jamin reluctantly pulled away from her mouth when he reached the stairs. He peppered kisses on her face as he climbed the stairs.

"You better not drop me, Jamin!" Shayla giggled, burying her head into his neck.

"Never." Jamin promised by the time he reached the landing at the top of the staircase. He had a firm grip on her round ass. When he effortlessly raised Shayla up and down across his manhood, her breath hitched sharply. He threw his head back, laughing. Bragging, Jamin walked into his bedroom. "I bench press your weight and more daily. You're the perfect fun size."

He set Shayla on the side of the king-size bed and took the bottles from her, placing them on the nightstand. Jamin watched her head spin around as if it were on a swivel to scope out his room. He could see the wheels turning in her head as she took in her surroundings. Once Shayla brought her eyes back to him, Jamin was on his haunches with her foot on his lap.

"Your room is, uhh, really nice, and like your kitchen, it's big."

He flashed a crooked grin. "It's not the only thing in here that's big. But thanks. I'll give you a tour of the rest of the house later."

"Okay." She let a nervous laugh and chewed her bottom lip. Her small hands clung to the edge of the bed.

The Weeknd's *High for This* filtered through the speakers in the background. Jamin locked his gaze on hers as he unhooked the buckle of her wedge sandal. He loosened the ankle strap and slid the sandal off her foot. Lifting it to his lips, Jamin kissed the inner side of her ankle. He took his time repeating the same with the other foot. After setting the sandals off to the side, he stood. He helped Shayla to her feet, guiding her to stand in front of him. Jamin pushed her shirt up, and Shayla helped with pulling it over her head. He reached skillful fingers behind her back and unfastened her bra with ease. Sliding the satin material down and off her arms, Jamin took a moment to admire the supple globes. He moistened his lips and lifted both with a husky whisper. "So soft and beautiful."

Compared to him, she was much shorter. Despite this, Jamin bent down and latched onto one of the dark brown tips, sucking hard. With his other hand, he rubbed, squeezed, and tweaked her nipple. She came up on her toes. He squished her breasts together, alternating between sucking and licking until her nipples were rigid peaks. Shayla's back bowed.

"Mmhmm." She pressed him closer to her bosom.

Jamin released one of her breasts and reached down to unbutton her pants. Once he unzipped them, he lifted his head. Slanting his mouth over hers, Jamin kissed her tenderly. He worked on removing her pants. Shayla raised her hips for him to push them down her thighs and legs. He retreated from her lips long enough to pull them off. The rosy scent from her pussy floated right into his nostrils. His dick twitched. Jamin rushed to pull his shirt off. He shucked his jeans off, relieving the tension on his dick. He cast a quick glance at Shayla. She gingerly moved a couple of steps back. She moistened her lips and fixated on the erected tent, which significantly extended the front of his boxer briefs.

Jamin chuckled, "Shayla baby, eyes up here."

Her eyes flitted up to meet his.

"You nervous?"

She quickly shook her head. Her eyes drifted below his waist again before she looked up and answered. "No … but you're far from average."

"Yeah, but I know you're going to handle every inch like a pro or tap out," Jamin reassured, taking a step to close the distance between them.

In a swift move, Jamin had a firm grip on her butt and lifted Shayla to his waist. She instinctively encircled his midsection with her thick thighs as she draped her arms around his neck. When her bottom lip caught his attention, Jamin couldn't help himself. Crushing his mouth on hers, the kiss was savage and possessive. He yearned for more. Jamin moved over to the bed and climbed on, easing Shayla on her back. He was careful not to put all his weight on her, extending the length of his body over hers. Separating her legs with his knees, he nestled himself between her thighs. He didn't pull away from their kiss. His hands fought over which of her soft curves he wanted to touch more. He alternated between caressing her breasts to massaging her ass as their bodies moved in sync with each other. Jamin reluctantly withdrew from her swollen lips. He began to plant kisses on her neck, moving down to the center of her stomach and pausing at the piercing in her belly button.

"This is sexy." He murmured against her stomach, twirling the jeweled butterfly.

Jamin hooked a finger at the top of her panties, tugging on them. Shayla lifted her hips, and he eased them down her legs until they were off. He was about to toss them, but hesitated. Instead, he brought the saturated seat of the thin fabric up to his nose and inhaled. Jamin's eyes rolled back until only the whites could be seen.

Shayla squealed, "Jamin! Are you ... oh my god, really?"

The heady scent of her pussy was unlike any other pussy he'd ever smelled before. It was the perfect fusion of her arousal mixed with a natural scent of musk. He knew it was heaven waiting inside of her silky walls. He refocused his eyes on her and let out a throaty laugh, seeing the crimson coloring on her cheeks. It was likely embarrassing to her but a complete turn-on for him. He glanced at her while licking the sweet essence from the seat.

Shayla squeezed her eyes shut and groaned. "And you're a perv. Ewww!"

"Nah uh, look at me. 'Cause you ain't seen shit yet, baby. We just getting started."

He waited for her to look. He nudged her thighs open wider with his shoulders. Jamin hooked his arms under her thighs, pinning her down. He stayed laser-focused on Shayla's eyes as his head dipped below. She whimpered when his tongue swiped across her drenched, vertical lips. His tongue split the swollen folds and slithered inside to sample the first blissful taste. Jamin knew he would be hooked. With his tongue buried inside the pink flesh, he used his thumb to rub her protruding bud.

Shayla fisted his locs with a firm hold as her legs shook uncontrollably. "Jamin!"

He adjusted his position between Shayla's thighs, gently bringing his arms out from under her. Jamin used his shoulder to keep her spread wide as he inserted a long, thick finger. Her tight walls clenched around it, urging him to go deeper. He pushed a second finger deep into the slick heat. Her pussy squeezed his fingers tighter, feeling as though she was going to break them off. She gyrated her hips on them, producing more of her creamy arousal, making it slippery wet. He curved his fingers upward to stroke her deep and slow. Her bundle of nerves swelled and appeared to cry out for him. Jamin dove in face first, as if it were his last plate of food. His tongue lashed back and forth and twirled around her drenched bud. Shayla arched her body to him.

"Oh my God, Jamin. Pleeease!" She rasped, thrashing her head back and forth across the bed.

He raised his head but continued to pump his fingers, and his thumb stroked her sweet berry as he demanded. "Please what?"

"Hmmm, it feels sooo good. Yes, that's it! That's it!"

"No, baby, tell me what you want." Jamin stopped finger fucking her and rubbing her clit.

She whined, reaching for his hand. "Nooo. Why'd you stop?"

He swatted her hand away and lowered his voice to a husky growl. "Use your words, Shayla. I wanna hear you say it."

She lowered her eyes and batted her lashes. He almost erupted in his boxers as she hush-whispered in the sexiest voice. "Pleeease Jamin... I-I want you to ... fuck me."

Jamin went to the nightstand for the condoms. He yanked his boxers off, ripped the gold wrapper open, and covered himself quickly. Climbing back on the bed, he settled between her thighs. Shayla opened them up wider. He gripped his shaft and rubbed the bulbous head across her folds, coating himself in her wetness. His heavy erection teased at her weeping entrance. She stretched her arms out to encircle his neck. Jamin lowered his mouth to hers, smothering her cries as he penetrated her snug, heated channel. Shayla was tighter than any fist. Although his shaft was only a few inches inside, it was already too much. Jamin was aware of his size and wanted to avoid hurting her, but the firm hold she had on his dick coaxed him to keep going. It was almost painful to work it in further. He withdrew a little, and with a slow stroke, eased in again. Deepening their kiss, he pushed another inch in, then paused and pushed again. He rolled his hips in slow circles, his girth stretching her open. She jutted her hips upwards to meet his stroke, and that did it. Shayla's nails dug into his back as he sank a couple more inches inside of her. Jasmine Sullivan's voice crooned out the lyrics to *BPW,* and Jamin retreated from Shayla's lips. Looking down where their bodies connected, he pulled out and watched how her body sucked him back in. He repeated the slow strokes. She writhed under him, moaning as he filled her completely. He groaned, easing out some, then slid back in.

"Fuck Shayla, you've got the best pussy in the world. And it's mine. You hear me, this pussy is mine." Jamin declared.

Shayla cried in response, "Yes! Yes!"

Their hearts pounded in sync as they moved together, their gazes locked on one another, their fingers entwined, and their bodies joined. He did his best not to lose himself in her wet warmth, but he couldn't help it. Her slick walls contracted and rippled all around him. The depth and speed of Jamin's strokes increased. He thought it was ironic The Dream's *Falsetto* echoed in the speakers around the same time her heavy breathing turned into high pitched screams. Jamin realized he'd begun to hit a tender region when Shayla pressed her hands against his thighs.

"Shit, baby. I'm 'bout to ..." He growled. The need to explode built up. A powerful sensation crept into his spine. His pumps became short and fast.

"Jamin!"

He gritted out, "Ahhh fffuck!"

His body tensed as he filled the condom. He went still for a moment, staying inside and letting her body milk him. Not wanting to disconnect from her, Jamin gathered her against his chest and rolled them over with Shayla on top. He ran his hands across her back. All that could be heard was their labored breathing and, in the background, Sabrina Claudio's *Unravel Me.* A few minutes later, Jamin withdrew from Shayla and turned them on the side. Jamin felt her body go rigid and noticed she winced when he pulled her close.

"You okay?"

She nodded quietly, keeping her gaze downward.

"Hey, look at me." To see her eyes, he squeezed her chin between his fingers and raised it. "I wasn't too rough, was I?"

She barely lifted her shoulders when their gazes met. "Kinda, but it's okay."

"No, it's not. Hang on. I'll be right back." He pressed a kiss on her forehead.

Jamin grabbed the throw from the end of his bed and covered Shayla. He went into the master bathroom and ran a soak bath. He retrieved shower gel, loofas, and towels from the linen closet. After adding essential oils to the water and lighting a few candles, he returned to the room. Without saying anything, he pushed the throw to the side, lifted Shayla from the bed bridal style, and carried her to the bathroom.

"Jamin, what are you—"

Her words faltered when she looked around the bathroom. She peered up at him and blushed. He gave a quick peck on the lips.

"Do you need to pee first?"

"Yes, please."

He carried her over to the water closet. After setting her on the floor, he waited for her to finish her business. When she came out, he lifted her in his arms again. He made his way over to the large soaking tub and placed her on the side. "Can you check to make sure it's good for you?"

Shayla eased her foot into the water and smiled. "Wow, it's perfect."

Jamin helped her inside, climbed in behind her, and brought her back to his chest. He wrapped her arms around her. He pressed his lips against her neck and murmured, "I'm sorry."

Shayla twisted her head to look up at him. "For what?"

"I could tell it hurt, Shayla, and I got a lil' rough. This should help with the soreness and your pH balance. My mom taught me a few things. I know how it is when you're with a new partner."

"Oh wow, okay."

Jamin could feel her body tense up while he spoke. Her lack of a response forced him to reveal another part of what she would have to be ready to deal with. He cupped her chin. "Hey, one thing you'll learn about me. I'm heavy on communication. I'm not shy, so when it comes to my woman, we're going to talk about this kinda stuff too."

"Wait, your woman?"

"Oh, you thought I was playing. That wasn't pillow talk, baby. I meant it when I said this the best pussy in the world. Yeah, this is mine and ain't nobody else sliding up in it. Understood?" Jamin reached between her thighs and slipped a finger between her folds.

Shayla gasped and leaned back. She rolled her hips, moaning. "Mmhmm, yes."

"That's my girl. Now let's soak this sweet pussy, 'cause I plan on stretching her out tonight."

CHAPTER 14

Yawning, Shayla extended her arms above her head. She winced from the soreness radiating throughout her body. It'd been a long time since she felt that kind of ache in her muscles. Another soak bath would be good. The previous evening with Jamin came to mind in an instant. Her mouth split into a naughty smile. She rolled over, bringing the sheet up to her nose. Her nostrils filled with Jamin's scent. He smelled so good. The sound of Jamin clearing his throat startled her. Shayla shot up so fast some of her hair tumbled in her face.

"Good morning. I hope I'm not interrupting anything," he greeted in an amused tone.

The flush crept into her cheeks. She couldn't help but feel embarrassed he'd caught her. Shayla swept her hair out of the way and laughed nervously. "Uhh no, I was just turning over. Hey, good morning."

"Uh huh, did you sleep good?"

"I did. Your bed is so soft."

"I know what else is soft." He strode over to her side of the bed.

Shayla eyeballed the tall, honey-colored god who was now her man. *My man. Oh-emmm-geee! Jamin Love is my man!* Even in loungewear, her man was sexy. She licked her lips. A black tank top stretched taut across his broad chest, displaying his tattooed, muscular arms. The lightweight cotton pants hung loosely at his waist. The adrenaline coursing through her veins was almost too much for her to handle. She swore he could hear her pussy purring its lusty good morning at the sight of his dick print. The bed dipped when he kneeled over her. She realized he was getting ready to kiss her.

Shayla jerked back and turned away. "No! I haven't brushed my teeth, Jamin."

He took hold of her chin, guiding her head back in his direction. He leaned in where their faces were inches apart. His warm, minty-fresh breath tickled her nose hairs. Her eyes zeroed in on his full pink lips as he murmured, "Do you think I care about your breath, seeing your pretty ass wrapped up in my sheets? Then I caught you sniffing them. It's obvious you missing your man." He paused and intently fixed his eyes on her mouth. His gaze was so intense that it felt like a million tiny lasers were being aimed at her lips. He slowly brushed his thumb across them. "Mmhmm ... listen Shayla, if I wanted some tongue, don't ever tell me no. You're mine now. And I have plans of getting very acquainted with *my* body. Every. Single. Inch. Make no mistakes about it, baby. I'm going to have you in every way imaginable."

She gulped hard. Her grip on the sheet tightened. An overenthusiastic response spilled from her pussy. Of course, she was excited and ready to get reacquainted with Jamin's dick. Her overzealous kitty greeted him with a wet welcome as soon as he walked in. The moisture pooled between her thighs. Shayla squeezed them together. Jamin grinned and wriggled the balled-up sheet from her fists. He peeled it back, exposing her naked body. She shuddered, but it wasn't from the temperature being cold. The desire for him scorched throughout her body. His piercing gaze and words had her shook. She knew Jamin meant what he said. The thoughts of all he would do to her, Shayla's pussy twitched. Her lips parted, letting out a soft moan.

Jamin gestured with a finger. "Spread 'em. Lemme see that pretty pussy."

She bit her nail while batting her eyelashes. Shayla seductively slid her other hand over her breast, stomach, and down to her thigh, pushing it open. Seeing Jamin's mouth damn near water did something to her. Shayla adjusted her position by digging her heels deeper into the mattress and widening her thighs. She squeezed her breasts together, lowered her head, and licked her nipples. Her eyes never left his. She'd never done anything risqué like it before, but Jamin watching her made Shayla feel sexy and uninhibited.

"Damn baby, you this wet for me?" he asked, dipping a finger into her delicate softness.

Shayla nodded, tucking her bottom lip into her mouth. He smiled as he withdrew the finger and thoroughly cleaned Shayla's arousal from it. Suddenly, his eyes darkened. Jamin lowered his head and let out an animalistic growl. He buried his face in her sex, savagely devouring Shayla as if he were starving and she was his first meal of the day. His tongue was going wild, sending wave after wave of pleasure through her body. The sensation of his tongue's powerful strokes sent her into a state of rapture. It was supposed to be the other way around, but when he locked on her clit and sucked, Shayla could feel him snatching her soul.

"Jaaaamin!" She cried out, crushing his head between her thighs.

He pried them open and pinned her thighs to the bed. Jamin inserted two fingers inside her pulsing channel. Curving them upward, thrusting in and out, Shayla could feel him stimulating her G-spot. The pad of his thumb rotated in a circular motion on her clit. He added a third finger, and she squirmed against him, holding on tight to his forearms. Jamin suctioned her sensitive bud in his mouth again. She was being tortured into delirium by his gifted mouth and tongue. She'd experienced a level of pleasure she had never known. Intense, hot sensations tingled and swirled below her waist. Her legs clenched, and she shook. Shayla screamed in release. Jamin withdrew his fingers, and hot liquid gushed from her body.

He sputtered, "Oh shit!"

Springing up in the bed, Shayla covered her mouth. She reached out for him but pulled her hand back. She held it up and expressed her remorse wholeheartedly. "Oh God, I'm-I'm so sorry, Jamin. I swear to you, I-I don't know what came over me, but that's never happened before."

After wiping his eyes and drying his beard with the sheet, Jamin looked up. His face revealed a wide grin before he affirmed. "Baby, there's nothing to be sorry for. I'm proud to know that I'm the first to make this happen for you."

Shayla's face contorted in confusion. Jamin got up from the bed. He went to the bathroom. She heard the water running. When he returned, he motioned for her to come to the edge of the bed. Like the night before, he cleaned her thoroughly. He went to return the washcloth and by the time he came back, she'd wrapped herself in the sheet again.

"Hey, what's that face for?"

Shayla lowered her eyes. Shaking her head back and forth, she picked at her cuticles. "No reason."

"Nah baby, look at me."

He told her it was nothing to be sorry for, but she couldn't help feeling embarrassed. She'd heard about it, but nothing like that had ever happened with anybody else. It felt weird. Shayla couldn't bring herself to look at him.

Jamin scooted closer. He hooked a smooth finger under her chin and lifted it. "Shayla baby, I need to see your eyes when I'm talking to you."

She chewed the inside of her jaw but forced her eyes up to meet his concerned gaze. He brushed the back of his hand down the side of her cheek, sending a flutter through her heart.

"So, lemme guess. You've never squirted before."

"No," she mumbled. She could feel her cheeks warming.

"God, you're so beautiful when you blush. Shayla baby, it's nothing to be ashamed about for real. If anything, I'm gonna need to get some waterproof sheets and weewee pads for this gushy pussy. You gon' be making some big messes in here."

"Really, Jamin?" She shoved him playfully.

He gathered her in his arms and nuzzled his face in her neck. "Hells yeah! Just saying, baby. I plan on making you squirt often."

"Oh my God!"

Her phone rang. Shayla glanced over at the nightstand. It was Lennie. As much as she wanted to ignore the call, she hadn't told her cousin where she was going the night before. Since they spoke every morning, she didn't want Lennie to worry about her. "Do you mind? I have to take this. Plus, I want to brush my teeth and wash my face."

"Yeah, your overnight bag is in the bathroom. You hungry?"

"Not really, but if you make something, I'm sure I'll eat."

He pressed a kiss on her forehead. "Okay, I'll see what I can whip up."

She waited for him to walk out before answering. "Hey, Lennie Bean."

"What's up, Shay Bae?"

Shayla purposely kept her face close to the screen as she got up from the bed. She padded to the bathroom. "Nothing. What you up to this morning?" Once she got to the water closet, she turned the camera off.

"Still trying to figure out what I'mma get into. But what happened to you yesterday? I thought we were gonna hit the mall after you finished up at the studio. Don't get me wrong. Jace came through, so I ended up thoroughly entertained."

Shayla finished her business and flushed. She went to the sink to wash her hands. She cleared her throat to confess. "I ended up with Jamin. And umm, I'm still at his house."

"What the hell did you just say?" Lennie exclaimed.

"You heard me." Shayla saw that he'd placed her bag on the bench ottoman in the sitting area. She unzipped it and pulled out the toiletry bag. She retrieved the mouthwash, toothpaste, and facial cleanser.

Lennie yelled, "Oh, hell no! That's why it's off? Turn that damn camera back on!"

"Hang on. Let me wash my face and brush my teeth."

"And you can turn it on to do all of that. Really, Shay Bae? The grouch's house?"

With a mouthful of the cool mint-flavored rinse, Shayla mumbled. "Uh huh."

"Did I miss something? How?"

Shayla ran some water and spit the mouthwash out. "Hold up, Lennie. Let me finish brushing my teeth."

"Nah uh. I wanna know why your camera not on. You have it on any other time at your house. What? You don't want me to see what the grouch got in there?" Lennie pressed with interest and curiosity.

Shayla lifted her head from the sink. She went to the bathroom door in a haste and closed it. The last thing she wanted was for Jamin to walk in and hear her cousin calling him that name. She caught her reflection in the mirror. Grabbing one of the plush towels from the shelf, Shayla covered her naked body. She set her phone on the tissue box and propped it up against the mirror. She turned the camera on. "Is that better?"

"Yes, much better." Her cousin said, leaning in with her eyes ping-ponging around to see Shayla's surroundings. "Oooh, his bathroom looks nice!"

Shayla shook her head while squirting a line of paste on the toothbrush. "You cannot tell that from this angle."

"I can so. He has some good taste, or some girl helped. 'Cause that dusty teal and white with the mocha accents are a good look."

She paused mid-stroke on her teeth and twisted her head to glance back at the bathroom décor. Leave it to her cousin to notice those details. His bathroom had a relaxing spa-like feel to it, but Shayla cringed thinking about that latter statement. She didn't want to think about another woman helping unless it was his mother. "Whatever," she mumbled, cutting her eyes at Lennie. She finished brushing her teeth and went through her face-washing ritual.

Lennie raised a brow. "Oooh, that's a big shower. Does it have jets?"

"Yes." Shayla confirmed applying moisturizer on her face. Next, she pulled her hair into a messy bun. She then applied a light gloss to her lips. Lastly, she took loungewear out and slipped it on.

"Now let me see everything. Take me on a tour of the master bath and his room!" Lennie demanded.

Shayla grumbled under her breath but grabbed her phone. She switched from the selfie to the camera view. Lennie's oohs and ahhs echoed from the device as she gave her cousin a quick tour of his large master bath.

Lennie declared, "I love that soaking tub. When I buy my dream house, I'm getting one!"

"It was so relaxing," Shayla said as she walked into his room. She showed Lennie the massive bedroom space, excluding the closet, to respect his privacy. She returned the view of the camera to herself and propped the phone up on her knees after sitting on the bed.

Lennie leaned in with her fingertips at her temples. "This is blowing my mind right now. You're at Jamin, the grouch's house!"

"He's not such a grouch after all." Shayla contradicted.

Her face was all the way in the phone when Lennie jested. "Oooh, lemme find out you got some grouchy dick!"

116

Shayla's eyes went to the door before she glanced down at the phone and giggled. "It was some bomb ass grouchy dick too."

Lennie's jaw dropped. She blinked several times. Shayla couldn't help laughing.

"No, seriously, you've gotta tell me what happened, Shay. What the hell did I miss?"

"Us doing the best cover I've heard of *Whenever You Call*. And him admitting that he's been trying hard not to like me." Shayla continued giving her cousin a condensed version of the day before at the studio when Jamin showed up. "And remember you thought something was up with how he acted around Christopher that day."

"Yeah, and last night Jace was hinting at it. Wow! Just look at you with the 'I got fucked good' face. You got that glow too! Mmhmm yasss, girl yasss!" A smile danced on Lennie's lips as she snapped twice.

"You are so dumb, girl."

Lennie's face twisted into confusion. She held up a finger. "Shay, does Jamin have music playing?"

Shayla frowned as Lil' Wayne's voice got louder in the background.

"Do you not hear that?"

She placed a hand over her mouth when Jamin opened the door with a big grin plastered on his face. He winked. At the same time, Shayla heard Lennie's question.

"Shay, is that *Tap Out*?"

Jamin came to the other side of the bed and climbed on. He sat next to her. Shayla moved her hand away, but her mouth hung open in shock at the audacity of his song selection. She sucked her teeth and rotated her neck. "Really?"

She poked her lips out. His eyes went right to them. Without hesitation or considering her cousin on the other end watching, he devoured them. Shayla let out a moan when Jamin slid his hand under her top and pinched her nipple. Lennie cleared her throat. Shayla and Jamin turned their attention to the phone in her lap.

"'Sup, Lennie, how you doing?" he greeted with a friendly smile.

"I'm good. And it looks like you are too. I'mma get outta y'all hair." She pointed at Shayla. "You, call me later. We need to finish this conversation, ma'am."

Then Lennie cocked her head to the side, shooting her a covert look. Shayla hesitated and chewed her bottom lip, but finally nodded. They sang their usual goodbye.

"Love you, Shay Bae."

"Love you more, Lennie Bean."

Shayla could feel Jamin's penetrating gaze on her when she ended the call. She leaned over to set her phone on the nightstand. He had changed his position on the bed and was now lying on his side. He'd propped himself up by the elbow. When she turned to face him, he motioned for Shayla to move closer. Jamin intertwined their legs. He brushed a knuckle across her cheek.

"That song you and Lennie were just singing, what's the name of it? Why did y'all sing it?"

"Always Be My Baby, and we always sing it when we tell each other goodbye. It's our cousin thing."

"You really like Mariah Carey, heh? Is that your favorite song by her?"

His eyes were on her lips again. If he hadn't told her they were his favorite feature of hers, she might have felt self-conscious about them. It was mutual. His lips were full and pink in shade. Jamin's thin mustache and anchor beard accentuated his full lips. He had a perfect, chiseled jawline. Shayla loved his natural sandy brown color locs. Some of them hung over his shoulder. She reached up and twirled a couple of locs between her fingers. "No, Fantasy is. And no, not the remix with Old Dirty Bastard. And I love her. She's my favorite artist."

"Yeah, how can I forget? I got that impression from day one."

"Hush." She pushed him in jest. "And who's your favorite?"

With a smug smile, he shared, "Prince."

"Ahh, the purple one. Why am I not surprised?"

"But do you know why?"

Shayla tapped her chin and beamed, "His fashion and style!"

"You've never seen me wear anything like him." Jamin scrunched up his face.

She tried her best not to laugh.

"Oh, you think that shit's funny. Come here," he said, pulling her closer and tickling her.

"Wait! Okay, okay, you dress way better. I swear. Stop, pleeease!" she begged. Shayla laughed hysterically. Tears began to form before he stopped.

"Now try again."

She calmed herself down and wiped her eyes. With a quick peck to his lips, she added, "He is one of the most prolific artists to date. I can see where you get some of your style of music from."

"Good save, but there's one more thing. I thought you would've gotten this. I guess you ain't been checking up on your man."

Shayla tugged on his arm, pleading in a whiny tone. "Okay, tell me, please, because I can't think of anything else you and Roger have in common."

"How about the day we were born?" he revealed.

Her eyes widened. "I mean, I knew, but it didn't click. You and Prince are Geminis! Wow, that's so freaking dope."

"Yeah, I think so too. My mom told me she thought about naming me after him, but my pops wasn't having it."

"What's wrong with Roger? When you get on my nerves, I could be like Tia and Tamera did Marques and tell you, go home, Roger!" she laughed so hard she snorted.

When her laughing subsided, she noticed Jamin staring at her. He rolled his eyes. "Really, Shayla?"

"Hey, be glad they didn't. But I think Prince would've worked. You're just as sexy."

"Absolutely not."

She giggled, thinking of how interesting it would've been if he'd been named after the artist. Her man was an amazing artist as well, but the contrasts between the two were obvious, and as it was, Jamin wouldn't be in anyone's shadow.

Shayla enjoyed learning things about him and looked forward to hearing more. A moment of silence fell between them as she snuggled closer. He squeezed her tight and gave her a quick peck.

"So, tell me what happened in NY four years ago."

Her body grew rigid. Shayla closed her eyes. It didn't surprise her Jamin asked. She knew it would come up. She'd expected it sooner. The issue was she dreaded reliving that day. Shutting down and repressing her emotions was easier. Shayla felt there was no need to dredge up the past. *What would be the point? I'm over it.*

"Baby?" Jamin's voice interrupted her from the mental battle.

She opened her eyes and sighed raggedly. "Yes."

"Would you prefer not to talk about it?"

Shayla wanted to tell him no, but he would likely bring it up again. She eased out of his embrace and sat up. Releasing a heavy sigh, she began sharing how her dream came true. "I made it as one of the finalists on *U Got Talent*. It was down to me, Tréy Legend, and this other girl, Akeela, Ameeka or whatever that chick name was. That night before, maybe I practiced too much. I don't know. But I felt fine all day. Drank tea and rested my voice until it was time for me to go on. Anyway, in front of a live audience of thousands singing the cover to *I Will Always Love You …*" Shayla paused. She gathered her knees to her chest, hugging them with her arms. There was a tremor in her voice as she continued. "The most embarrassing moment of my singing career happened. Went for that first high note, and my voice cracked. After all my vocal training, nothing could prepare me for that. I didn't recover fast enough. It was the stares. It was the silence. Ugh, that deafening silence got so loud, Jamin. Panic settled in, and I bolted from the stage. With it being a reality show, the mics were on, and the cameramen captured it all. The producers had questions. You know they followed me off stage, asking what was wrong and what happened, but I couldn't say anything. What could I say? I ripped the mic box off and didn't turn around. I kept going. I remember leaving the auditorium. Somehow, I made it back to the hotel. I called Lennie and my parents because I just didn't want to be there anymore. So, I came home. That was it. I quit. I fucking quit."

Her chest heaved. Releasing a quiet sob, the tears that Shayla didn't know were there, now flowed free and streamed down her cheeks. She tried swiping them away, but more fell. Jamin didn't say anything. He got up from the bed. A few moments later, he returned with some tissue.

Shayla took them from him. She wiped her face and sniffled. "It's okay to cry you know."

"I know, baby." He sat next to her and began rubbing circles in the middle of her back.

"Why did you bring it up? What, you think I won't be able to handle the pressure or something? You think I'm gonna quit when we get to Vegas?" she choked out angrily.

His brows furrowed. Jamin stopped rubbing her back. He scooped Shayla up and placed her on his lap. He kissed her forehead and cradled her to his chest like a baby. "You didn't hear me say any of that. I brought it up 'cause I'm nosey and wanted to know what happened. You said you didn't want to be there, right?"

Shayla barely nodded in response.

Jamin tilted his head and stared into her eyes with intensity. "Hey, it took a lot of hard work and effort for you to make it as a finalist, right? Months and months, no? You ain't give up on your career, even if it meant taking a break from music for a minute. Think of this as the perfect opportunity that was waiting for you to be here with me. Hell yeah, it was tough for me to accept at first, but I knew from the door you were the one. Not just in terms of music, either. Yeah, there are far more reasons than that why you're here now. I already told you what I look forward to daily, and a nigga ain't trying to lose this. And you won't quit when we get to Vegas 'cause I'll be there. Okay, let's say your voice does crack. You won't be able to run off the stage. 'Cause I won't let you." He kissed her tear-stained cheeks.

Shayla heard him, but wished she could hide the feeling of vulnerability that came with the conversation. It was an uncomfortable topic. She hated breaking down in front of him, but knowing that he was on her side, and offering support, it gave her some comfort. With everything he'd said, there was something that now made Shayla curious. She opened her mouth to ask but stopped and looked away, sighing.

"What?" he probed.

She wasn't sure if it was the right time to bring it up. Shayla's focus shifted to one of the long locs near her hand, which she began twirling between her fingers. If he could draw out such a difficult truth from her, it was time for him to reveal his own. She turned her head to face his inquisitive chestnut irises and spoke openly. "They said you've changed since Cami passed. If I had to guess, y'all were close like Lennie and me, eh? Losing your cousin like that, I would think it'd be hard to be the same. How could you be? Anyway, Ursula said you needed to stop blaming yourself. What did she mean by that? What happened that night? I read the articles, but you know how it is getting information from the media outlets. It's secondhand and, more often than not, a stretch from the truth."

Shayla regretted her words as soon as Jamin lifted her from his lap and set her on the bed. He scooted to the head of the bed and leaned against the headboard, scrunching his face in frustration.

"Okay, that was out of pocket, right? Right. It's too soon for me to be all up in your business like that. I'm sorry. I just thought because we were sharing, well, I was and, well, you know. But I get it that it's probably too much to go into being the nature of how she passed and shit. Look, I shouldn't've asked, that was my bad and—"

He leaned in, and with his index finger cradling her chin, he locked eyes with her and smirked. "Shayla baby, are you gonna let me answer?"

She gave a little nervous chuckle. "Yes, sorry."

Jamin straightened his posture, pulled his hair back away from his face, inhaled a long breath, and started talking. "Yeah, we were a lot like you and Lennie. Cami's mom is my mom's younger sister. They were pregnant with us at the same time too. I was born a month before that ball of fire. My baby cousin was a light to everybody around her. Minus that snort, like yours, her laugh was infectious. She could brighten up the darkest of rooms just with her laughter. And I don't care who it was, she always found the good in everybody. She lived her life on the edge and was carefree. Most of all, yeah, like you, Cam could sing her ass off too." He stopped speaking for a moment, his eyes shining with emotion. Tears were threatening to spill over the edges of his eyelids. He inhaled deeply again and continued. "It was another release party for our last album. Everybody was drinking and having a good time. I saw some asshole who'd been trying to get at her all night. I stepped in, but she told me she was good and didn't need me watching over her. Somehow, Cam slipped away with this guy who I knew had too much to drink. And well, you know the rest. They found the car wrapped around a telephone pole about five miles away from the club. Life can be cruel, heartless, and unapologetic. I'd never lost someone so close. You can never be ready to lose the people you love. What's crazy is that you're a lot like her, Cam. I mean a whole helluva lot, which is why I know I was trying hard not to like you. And it's not that I blame myself. But it's just that I should've paid closer attention, the same as I did for you last night. Knowing what I'd heard, I damn sure wasn't about to let that shit go down again on my watch. Couldn't risk that shit. Not again and not with you."

He finished, and the tears that'd been gathering in his eyes spilled over. Shayla moved to her knees and cradled his face between her hands, planting kisses on his wet cheeks. "Oh Jamin, I'm so sorry for your loss."

He bowed his head, shedding more tears. "I miss her."

Shayla wrapped her arms around him, embracing him to her chest and holding him tight. "I know I can never fill the void she left in your heart. But if I can bring even a small glimmer of light into your world, then I'll do all I can to make sure it stays there for you."

A few minutes passed before Jamin eased from her embrace and guided her to straddle his lap. "Shayla baby, you fill my life with a light so bright that I can't get enough of it." He peered down and chuckled. "And since I ain't never gon' sample Lela Rochon's to confirm it, I know this right here is the real deal sunshine."

She playfully shoved him. "Shut up."

"I'm dead ass though." Jamin paused for a few seconds, studying her face. He softly said, "Thank you, Ms. Sunshine." Then, he bent his head and sucked her bottom lip into his mouth.

Shayla moaned, flinging her arms around his neck. She grabbed a handful of his locs and tangled her fingers in it. When she rolled her hips into his growing package, Jamin groaned and eased from her mouth.

He rested his forehead against hers. "Nah uh, not yet. I came in here and got distracted. You need to eat first. I could tell your ass was acting hangry a minute ago, yelling at me."

"No, I wasn't!" Pushing her lips to pout, Shayla whined.

Jamin got up with Shayla in his arms. He wrapped her legs around his waist as he gave her a quick peck on the nose as he headed out of the room. "Look at how you're pouting and whining now. Yeah, lemme put some food in your belly before I fill you up with this dick."

CHAPTER 15

Hey babe ... wow. I still can't believe I get to call you that now. I was just thinking about the past few days. I don't think I said it, but thank you. Not only do you make some bomb-ass French toast, you give good back rubs. Annnnd OMG, you're the best lover ever! Thank goodness for those soak baths to keep my pH balanced ;-) Well, that's it. I'm on my way – **Shayla**

As soon as her name flashed across his cell's display, Jamin's heart swelled. He read the text message and chuckled to himself. Shayla's radiant energy and upbeat attitude were infectious. Jamin made it his mission to do whatever it took to keep her smiling. The other day, when she shared her most embarrassing moment and cried, he wished he'd been there to encourage and be the support she needed. In disclosing a lot about themselves to one another over the past few days, his feelings for her deepened. He hadn't felt this way about anyone else. He cared a lot about Kelly, but Shayla infiltrated his heart and planted herself inside. Although it was a new relationship, Jamin knew there would be no one else for him. Shayla was the one. He grinned hard while keying in his response.

Of course, baby, you're welcome. And believe it cuz I'm yours and you're mine. Now, hurry up. I need my tea – **Jamin**

> I got it and would've been there by now, but you told me to leave my truck at home. Lennie picked me up late. See you soon *kisses* – **Shayla**

He, Jace, and Zayne were in a huddle at the piano discussing the music for the evening when he heard her bubbly voice bellow out a greeting to Daria. Jamin glanced up for a brief second, but he had to do a double take. His mouth flew open when he looked up again and gave his complete attention to Shayla. If it were any lower, his jaw would've hit the floor. She had gone for a new look, trading in her usual natural curly hair or faux locs for a glamorous blowout with bouncy spirals that fell past her shoulders. The red, off-the-shoulder, bodycon dress she wore hugged her curves in all the right places, showing off her slim-thick figure. Her red bottom nude sandals had spike embellishments on the cross straps and a wide clasp that curved around her ankles, giving the appearance her legs were longer and more muscular. She was breathtakingly beautiful. Jamin's dick agreed, thumping in appreciation at the stunning sight.

"You might wanna close your mouth before a bug flies in it." Jace joked.

Jamin gave him a playful elbow to the ribs. "Man, shut up."

Daria teasingly chided Shayla for dressing better than her. He returned his attention to the ladies when he heard Shayla's infectious laugh. Jamin couldn't help it. *That dimple.* As soon as she opened her mouth, his eyes shifted to her full, pouty lips coated in gloss.

Shayla gestured up and down with her hand. "You are looking fierce in this dress. And these thigh-high boots! Daria girl, please. Is she being serious right now, Len? She can't be."

"I'm not talking to Lennie either. That bitch never fails on her fits. Look at all that ass y'all carrying in them dresses. Ugh. Y'all cousins make me sick!"

They exchanged looks, then burst out laughing as they complimented each other on how well they had pulled off their different styles. Shayla finally turned her head in his direction and saw him watching her. She excused herself from the ladies, sauntered over to the piano, and handed him the cup.

He gave her a slow once over. As much as he wanted to pull her into his arms, Jamin restrained himself. He winked, taking the cup from her. "Thanks. I 'preciate it."

She bit her bottom lip and gushed. "No problem. You're welcome."

"Hold up, that's who you were texting? She brought you tea and didn't get us nothing? Bruhhh," Zayne grunted in disbelief.

Jace held up his hand. "Hol' up, newbie. I thought you wasn't gon' be no runner. Who always has your back when Oscar here gives you all the smoke? How you do me like that?"

Jamin hoped he wouldn't have to wait until later to touch her. Seeing it was the perfect opportunity, he swept her into his arms. "Aye, y'all not gon' be ganging up on my girl like this. I ain't tell her to bring y'all nothing 'cause y'all asses already had drinks in your cups and didn't bring me nothing."

"Your girl?" Jace, Zayne, and Daria asked in unison.

Lennie snorted. "Yep. Aren't they cute together?"

"You knew and didn't tell me?" Jace's eyes bugged.

Lennie shrugged. "Wasn't my place to. And see, he's telling y'all now."

Jamin cocked his head in Lennie's direction and smirked. He peered down at Shayla, whose cheeks were now stained in scarlet. Quickly lowering her eyes, she began chewing on her bottom lip. The worried lines on her forehead didn't get past him. He gripped her chin, lifting it so she could see his eyes. With a slight shake of the head and a reassuring glance, he conveyed a silent message. He needed her to know and feel their relationship would always be safe around his friends. She finally nodded. His gaze moved to her lips, and he couldn't resist. Using his thumb, he pulled the bottom lip from her mouth. A pulse shot through his dick, making him shudder. He snapped his head up to look away before he ravished her in front of everybody. Jamin returned the focus back to his friends. Clearing his throat, he confirmed with confidence. "Yeah, Shayla's my girl, my lady, my woman."

"Honestly, it's about damn time," Daria praised.

Zayne nodded. "Yeah, 'cause you were running us ragged with your mood swings."

"The fuck you mean, I ain't have no mood swings," Jamin argued.

Jace snorted. "Like hell you didn't. You're already a moody motherfucka as it is. It got worse 'cause you was liking Shayla, but you didn't want to. Tell me I'm lying, that you and Shayla wasn't feeling each other since day one. Shit, we been waiting for y'all to figure this shit out."

"Facts," Lennie added.

Jamin peeked down at Shayla. She shrugged. "You know they're right, Oscar."

He leaned in and growled, "Don't worry, I'mma make sure you squirt all over this grouchy dick later." She tried to say something, but he covered her mouth with his lips.

"Awww! Too cute. We're so happy for y'all!" Their friends cheered and chorused in support.

Jamin reined everybody in from the distraction to prepare for their show. It would be starting soon. He resumed going over the itinerary for the evening and decided to put in a request with the group. "Umm, wanna run something by y'all. Shayla and me got this song. What y'all think about us adding it to the lineup?"

"Wait, is this for real a song, song? You singing? A whole song?" Jace joked when he checked the music sheet.

Jamin retorted. "Yeah, nigga. Just be ready for your part."

"Oh no doubt, this feels like a banga. You wrote it, Jamin?" Zayne asked while reviewing it.

He nodded in Shayla's direction. "With my baby's help, yeah."

Like he knew would happen, Shayla's cheeks flushed. She had no reason to be modest. The song was poetic in a brilliant way. Its lyrics described what it felt like to lose a love that seemed like it would endure forever before meeting the person they were meant to be with. He'd been in a dark space, or as Jace said, down in that can since Cami passed. Like the sun, Shayla appeared and brought light into his life. A low hissing sound from the cymbal and the drum rolling jolted Jamin out of his thoughts.

"Get your head outta the clouds, Jay!" Jace bobbed his head, drumming the opening beat. He pounded the drums vigorously to egg Jamin on. "It's time to get this one down. Yeah, I'm feeling it."

Jamin slid onto the bench, laughing. His attention went to center stage. He winked at Shayla while his fingers glided across the keys playing his favorite melody and stated, "LMK, it's time to give the people what they want."

Hours later, the group ended their show to a standing ovation and an overwhelming request for an encore song. Jazzmine, who was also a huge fan of theirs, was unable to refuse. After the final song, they headed upstairs to the VIP room for a meet and greet with their fans.

Once they were inside the large space, Jamin relaxed seeing a small crowd. He didn't want to spend more than an hour catering to these strangers. His plans for the night involved getting Shayla out of her dress. As if she'd heard his thoughts, she looked right at him. Her eyes widened and her mouth opened in disbelief. She'd caught him bringing his gaze up from her backside. She mouthed the word 'creep' and returned her attention to one of their fans standing in front of her. He chuckled to himself. If she was anywhere near him, Jamin would be a creep. As sexy as his woman was, he couldn't help ogling at her. He decided to put some space between them and headed to the other side of the room.

As Jamin had hoped, the next hour flew by, taking pictures and signing autographs. The club had opened to its usual patrons. By the time they were finished, some of them moved into the VIP area. Someone standing in the corner on the other side of the room caught his attention right as Jace stood in front of him.

"So, what y'all getting into after this?"

"Nothing. Going back to my house." Jamin answered in a tone more rushed than he intended. He peered over Jace's shoulder and frowned. The person he thought was Kelly a moment ago wasn't there. During the show, he thought he'd seen her in the crowd too. They hadn't spoken since that night of the release party. He hadn't planned on it, but she frequently hung out at their events to hook up with him afterwards. Now that he was with Shayla, Jamin needed to cut her off.

Jace waved a hand in his face. "Aye Jay, you cooking?"

"Not for you."

"Come on yo. How you gonna do us like that?"

Jamin arched an eyebrow. "*Us?* Who is us?"

Zayne came up beside Jace, draping an arm around his shoulder. Shayla and Lennie joined them, as well as Daria. Jace revealed a big grin. He opened his hands wide. "Nigga, *us.* Yo, Zayne, Daria, y'all see this. Your boy acting brand new. He ain't cooking for us."

Daria pushed her lips out and whined, "Is he for real, Jamin? You not cooking for us tonight?"

"Nope, not tonight." Jamin rocked his head from side to side. He extended a hand to Shayla. She grabbed it, and he drew her over to him. "Y'all niggas betta figure something out. Me and my baby 'bout to be out. And I ain't playing, Jace. Don't bring your ass to my house."

Jace jerked his head back in shock. He put a hand on his chest. "Wooow, this nigga gon' do his fam dirty over a new chick."

"Nigga, you gon' make me—"

"Damn, Jay, relax! You know I'm just fucking with you. We had plans to kick it here. The way you can't keep your eyes off Shayla, we already knew y'all was gon' be out."

"Then we out. See y'all next week." Jamin replied over his shoulder as he turned and guided Shayla out the rear exit door.

Without exceeding the speed limit, he made it home in record time. Jamin shifted the gear into park and peeked over at Shayla, who smiled back. He kissed the back of her hand. As bad as he wanted to ravish her on the ride there, he settled for holding her hand so he could focus on the road. He had to refrain from touching her. The things he wanted to do required more room than the front seat could provide. He hopped out and rounded the SUV in seconds. Jamin flung the passenger door open and scooped Shayla from the seat. Given that her dress would come off soon, he no longer gave a damn about it. He wrapped her legs around his waist. As he repositioned her in his arms so he could maneuver better, the tip of his dick jabbed her.

"Jamin!" she gasped.

He closed the passenger door with a devilish grin. His eyes went to her lips. "Yeah baby."

"Your dick, it's ... you're poking me in my ass." She lowered her eyes seductively.

When she slid her tongue out and swiped it across her lips, Jamin covered her mouth with his. In a hurry to get into the house, he nearly broke his key off in the garage door. Loud, continuous beeps came from the alarm system. Jamin didn't withdraw from their sloppy tongue kiss while heading over to the wall where the alarm's panel was. Pressing her back against the wall next to the box, he eased from her lips. He felt an immediate loss. Her sweet kisses were like a drug, and he was a fiend. He needed more. After getting a few more pecks in, he finally focused on the panel. He had to or else the alarm would go off.

Jamin keyed in the code to disarm it. The system announced it'd been disabled. His eyes swung back to the beautiful woman pinned against his wall. A low moan escaped from Shayla. The beast mode in him activated in response to the sound. He kissed, nibbled, and sucked on her hot skin, working his way down her neck. His teeth scraped across her shoulder. His hands explored, grabbing and massaging her voluptuous curves. He yanked the top of her dress down, exposing her breasts. He fondled the supple globes, alternating between both nipples, sucking and tugging until they hardened into turgid peaks.

"Yesss." Shayla hissed.

Jamin hovered over her luscious, pouty lips. He would never deny his attraction to them. His tongue split the seam and slithered inside. Their tongues twisted and entwined, savoring each other's mouths. Shayla tightened her grip on his locs. Moving her hips, she grazed against his stiff erection as their passionate kiss deepened. His dick began to ache with the need to slide between her heated walls. Jamin groaned, withdrawing from her swollen lips. He rested his forehead against hers. Shayla's dress had bunched up around her waist, revealing a black lace thong. Reaching a hand between her thighs, his long fingers brushed across the seat. She'd soaked through them completely. Her brown eyes were glazed with desire.

"Shayla baby, you're so wet, and the way you looking at me … damn girl. I wanna make love, but nah, you getting fucked," he mumbled against her lips.

Her breath was a hot caress on his. "Then what are you waiting for? Fuck me, Jamin."

His heart thudded out of his chest as he thought about what he wanted. He'd never done it before, but he wanted to connect with Shayla in a special way. He set her on the floor. Jamin took a deep breath and confessed, "I want you so bad right now, but I don't want no barriers between us, baby. I ain't never been with a girl raw. I get checked out annually and can show you my recent tests. I'm not saying I want us to have a baby right now. I just need to know this is gonna be me and you from here on out 'cause … fuck Shayla, you're it for me. Tell me you—"

Shayla put a finger to his lips. "Jamin, I have an IUD. I get checkups annually as well. I'll share my recent test results. And there's no one else. You're it for me too, babe."

That was all he needed to hear. His eyes didn't leave hers while he came out of his shoes and unbuttoned his pants. He shoved them down along with his boxers. Kicking them away, Jamin reached between her legs and ripped the flimsy lace material away. He bent down, cupping her ass cheeks, and in one swift move, he picked Shayla up. Her legs dangled over his forearms. Shayla held onto his neck. Their gazes remained on each other as Jamin eased her onto his throbbing shaft. She whimpered as he pushed the head of his dick and a couple of inches inside the slippery heat. Her velvety walls clenched down, coaxing him to go further. She was a snug fit, but his girth would stretch her. He pulled out a bit and dropped lower in his stance. Pressing her back into the wall, he plunged deeper. Shayla screamed. He paused to kiss and apologize for hurting her. She shook her head while rotating her hips in circles on his dick.

"It's a hurt so good, baby. Please fuck me, Jamin. Pleeease!" she begged.

He gripped her ass tighter, moving inside, working her open. Her smoldering, slick pussy rippled and clamped around his dick. Jamin thrusted his hips upward into her womb, losing himself in the warmth.

She cried out his name. "Jaaamin!"

He grunted, "Shayla baby, you keep squeezing my dick like this, you gon' make me bust."

"I can't … I can't help … oooh, Jamin! Baby, oh god I'm coming! I'm coming!"

Her body stiffened, and her legs began to shake. Warm liquid dripped down Jamin's balls and thighs as Shayla's slick channel clenched him tighter. Not only had she squirted, but she'd also had an orgasm. The sensation he'd fought off moments earlier he couldn't keep at bay anymore. He now chased after his own orgasm. He pumped harder and faster before stopping abruptly. The pleasure paralyzed him. Jamin shot his seed into her with the force of a storm. Panting heavily, he rested his damp forehead against hers. Their breaths mingled in an intimate confession. He knew this was right. Never had a woman felt so good, so perfect. She was home.

"Shayla baby, that was fucking amazing! You're so beautiful. Sexy. Mine." Jamin murmured between light smooches on her lips.

"Mmhmm, and you're my sexy grouch."

"Uh huh, I'm gonna make sure I keep you full of this grouchy dick too." Jamin gave her another quick peck. He brought her legs down, placing her on the floor. "Come on. Let's get cleaned up. I'm gonna cook us something. You gonna need sustenance for later."

He bent down for his clothes. Shayla grabbed his arm. "Babe, when you rushed us out, I forgot to get my bag from Lennie's car. I don't have anything to change into."

"Get her to drop it off when they leave Jazzmine's. You can put on one of my tees in the meantime. I'm sure it'll be like a dress on you."

What Jamin intended to be a quick shower turned into another session, with Shayla pinned against the wall when she bent over to pick up her loofa. He couldn't resist dipping in Shayla's honey pot again. After showering, they dressed and returned downstairs so he could begin cooking dinner. Shayla took a seat at the oversized breakfast island while Jamin went to get the pans he needed from underneath the cabinet.

"Are you making me one of your signature dishes?"

He responded from behind the refrigerator door. "As a matter of fact, I am. Get ready to enjoy the best stir-fry beef you've ever had this side of Atlanta."

"If it's by my man, Chef-Boyard-Jay, I already know it's gonna be delicious! The French toast you made the other morning was bomb, babe. Oh-emmm-geee! I can still taste the cinnamon. Mmhmm, yummy in my tummy." She licked her lips whilst making circles on her stomach.

Jamin pointed the knife, warning her in a low growl, "Dammit Shayla, make that noise and lick your lips like that again. I ain't cooking shit. I'll be fucking you right here on this island instead."

She giggled. "Sorry. Is there anything I can help you with?"

"Yeah, you can get the wine out. Let's go with a white one. It's a Reisling on the top shelf I think you'd like. I remember you said not too sweet and not too dry. Pour us a glass, sit there and be pretty."

Jamin chopped the vegetables. Shayla got the glasses from the cabinet and the bottle from the refrigerator, where he kept the alcohol chilling. She brought everything back to the island. After pouring, she took a sip. She covered her mouth, catching herself mid moan.

"Shayla baby, you think I'm playing. I have no problem putting you over my knee."

She picked up her phone rather than meeting his threatening glare. "Hey Lennie Bean. Can you drop my bag off at Jamin's house? I forgot to grab it when we were leaving. I'll text you the exact address."

Her cousin's voice was loud coming from the other end. "I called you! We was just about to leave! Where's Jamin?"

Shayla held the phone away. "Why are you being so loud? You drunk? He's right here about to cook for me."

"Oh good. I can get me a plate." Lennie leaned in. Although she tried to whisper, her voice was still loud. "Promise I won't tell the rest of them. And no, I ain't drunk. Okay, maybe a lil' tipsy. Anyway, tell him to call Jace. He's been trying to call him for the last ten or fifteen minutes. He said it's important."

"Where he at? Put 'em on." Jamin asked as he finished cutting the vegetables. He walked over to the sink to wash his hands.

Lennie hiccupped. "He went to the bathroom. I'll tell him to call you when he gets out."

It was then Jamin noticed his phone wasn't on the counter or the island. He shoved his hands in the pockets of his basketball shorts, but they were empty.

"I guess we'll be on our way when he comes out. See y'all in a few."

While Shayla sang goodbye to her cousin, Jamin headed out to the garage. He rummaged through the console in his truck, but it wasn't there either. He checked the counter by the door when he came back into the kitchen. Jamin rubbed the side of his temple. His forehead wrinkled.

"What is it, babe?"

"I can't find my phone."

Shayla got up from the island. "Where was the last place you had it? We've only been down here and upstairs."

Jamin snapped his fingers. "My pants' pocket upstairs. I never took it out when we went up to take a shower." On his way out, he stopped mid-step. He pivoted on his heel, trotted back over to her, and bent down to kiss her. Jamin backed away, pointing an accusatory finger. "Woman, you are a distraction."

Shayla giggled. "I can't focus when you're around either."

He exited the kitchen and climbed the stairs two at a time. Once he made it to his room, he looked around. Remembering he'd thrown the pants in the hamper, Jamin went to the walk-in closet. He took them from the basket and retrieved his phone from the pants pocket. Right away, he knew why he hadn't heard the ringing. The phone was set to vibrate. He frowned. Jamin got an eerie feeling after seeing he'd missed more than a dozen calls from Jace. He swiped across the screen to return his best friend's call.

"Where the fuck you at?" Jace demanded without so much as a greeting.

"Home. Why you called me that many times? What happened?"

"Kels, nigga."

As soon as he heard her name, his brows knitted together. "Huh?"

"You heard me. She was here looking for you and was pissed you left."

Jamin knew he'd seen her earlier. She intended to come over for sex as usual. He'd planned to cut her off after that last time. Those days were unquestionably behind him, now that he was with Shayla. He walked out of the closet.

"I was trying to give you the heads up she prolly gonna pop—"

"Hol' up, Jace. Shit, she's here!" Hearing their exchange, his eyes grew big.

What are you doing here?

Isn't it obvious? Now why are you here? No, better yet. How did you even get in?

See, that's how I know you're clueless about us. We have history, girl. Three years' worth.

Oh, I know about your history, Kels.

Kelly! That's what my name is.

Whatever.

Do you really think he wants you?

Think? Ha! I already know he got what he wants. Me.

Hmph, it won't be for long if I have anything to do with it.

Girl, please. You said it yourself. Y'all have history. We're together now. I'm his future.

Like hell you are!

I ain't going nowhere. So, what are you gonna do about it?

I oughta—

Jamin reached the kitchen in time to see Kelly moving toward Shayla. There was no way he would allow them to fight and not about him, especially when he was supposed to end things with Kelly, so nothing like this would happen. He wedged himself between the two women with his back facing Shayla. Reaching behind, he wrapped an arm around her waist, drawing her up against him and guiding her to take a few steps back. He pointed a finger, chiding Kelly. "Yo, what the fuck is wrong with you?"

"No, what the fuck is wrong with you? I was waiting for you, but Jace said you left. So, I came to see why you ain't been returning my calls. Now I know. What the fuck is *she* doing here?"

He'd allowed Kelly to get too comfortable. It was clear she'd forgotten their rules of engagement. Her emotions led her to make this mistake. Jamin let out a sardonic laugh. "Ain't nothing wrong with me. Last I checked, your ass is in *my* house. You don't get to ask about nobody I invited to be here. And I don't recall inviting you to come over. You know damn well I ain't with the pop-ups."

"Then you should've changed the damn code." He frowned and was about to respond, but Kelly craned her neck to look around him. She pointed at Shayla. "And that's who you want over me?"

"Yo, what you not about to do is disrespect my girl."

She retorted. "*Your* girl?"

Shayla slipped out of his arm. He turned around and stuck his arm out, blocking her path. "Hold up. Where you going?"

"Seems like you two have a lot to talk about."

"Shayla baby, I asked where you going? No, better yet. How you leaving here?"

She cocked her head and shot him a frosty glare. "Home, and I'm getting an Uber."

"No, the f—" Jamin looked up at the ceiling. Of all things to happen tonight. He hadn't planned on ever having his ex-girl confront his new girl. Shayla was everything he needed and wanted, not Kelly. It wasn't fair to Shayla he didn't handle the situation sooner and was now on the receiving end of Kelly's tantrum. Jamin wasn't about to let Kelly ruin his relationship before it even got started. He let out a harsh breath and whirled around to face her. His lips drew back in a snarl. "I swear I'm trying, Kels. You know I'm not that nigga who wilds out. But you 'bout to make this shit ugly. Do you really wanna do this? I'm telling you, this shit ain't gonna be pretty if I go there. I suggest you leave now."

He watched her lower lip quiver, the tears well, and her attempt to blink them back. Jamin wasn't moved by the crocodile tears. He cut his eyes from

Kelly and returned his attention to Shayla. His demeanor shifted. He forced an uncomfortable smile. Jamin grabbed hold of her arms. "Shayla, baby, I'm truly sorry about this. I should've taken care of it weeks ago, so nothing like this would've happened. She don't mean nothing to me. I swear."

Kelly's voice shrilled from behind. "What you mean, I don't mean nothing to you! Are you being for real right now, Jamin? Who else you been fucking with all this time then? I was there for you when Cami died! Don't that count for something? After everything we been through, you wanna throw it away for her? Who the fuck is she? What she got that I don't, huh? Nah uh, I'm not going out like that. It's been you and me for almost three years! She just got here. So, I know she don't know you like I do!"

Jamin closed his eyes for a brief second. He tried to center himself. Opening his eyes, he peered down at the luscious lips he'd fallen in love with. He hooked a finger under her chin, tilting her head back. Leaning forward, he brushed a soft kiss across her lips. "Shayla baby, I'm sorry you have to see me like this. I tried to be nice about it. I swear I never wanted this to ever go down. This ain't how I move. Gimme a minute 'cause I promised you the best stir fry in Atlanta. Tomorrow bomb-ass French toast, okay? And as much grouchy dick as you can handle. Just don't leave."

Her cheeks flushed, but she silently bobbed her head.

He lowered his eyes and released a heavy sigh. Jamin spun around and made a beeline for Kelly. The expression on his face must've made it clear he wasn't open to discussing anything else with her. Kelly's eyes bulged. She stumbled backwards out the kitchen as he unleashed on her. "What the fuck you thought this was, Kels? A relationship? I told you long time ago that shit was never going to happen again. And you know exactly why. Did you think I'd forget that fuck shit you did to me? Everything we been through? Nah, *you* took me through some bullshit. Hell yeah, I'd throw it all away. The fuck you take me for, Kels, a simp? You don't get to bring Cami up in this. She never liked your ass, anyway. Oh, you wanna know what my girl has? Everything you don't got. Most of all, the best pussy in this world. Now, it didn't even have to go down like this. 'Cause I ain't ask you to come over."

"Jamin, please," she reached out, pleading.

His nostrils flared. He knocked her hands away. "Nah, you brought your ass over here thinking it was gonna go your way. But you knew how this shit was from the door. No need in acting like we got more than we do. What we had was dead the day you let that other nigga bust in you and you had his seed."

Kelly slammed into the wall next to the door. The tears rolled down her cheeks. There wasn't a sympathetic bone in Jamin's body. She tried to reach out for him again. Jamin jerked away, glaring at her. He grabbed the doorknob and swung the door open.

Through sobs, Kelly choked out, "I'm so sorry, Jamin."

"Time to go. Bye, Kels."

She let her head drop. Kelly took her time walking out. She made it a few steps down the walkway before turning around. "Jamin, I just wish you would—"

He slammed the door. Jamin whipped out his phone, opened the app, and trotted back to the kitchen. "Shayla baby!"

CHAPTER 16

Jamin came into the kitchen and saw Shayla sitting at the island. She had the glass turned up, finishing off the remaining wine. She'd agreed to stay. He was grateful she did. She didn't have to. Right now, he needed to take care of an important detail. He slowed his stride as he approached the island. She hadn't acknowledged him yet. "Shayla baby?"

Shayla set the empty glass on the island countertop. She grabbed the wine bottle and replenished her glass with the golden liquid. She took a quenching sip, then placed the half-full glass down in front of her. Twisting her head in his direction, Jamin could see she'd applied more gloss to her lips. *Damn.* His dick pulsed happily. He loved that shit too. She finally addressed him, "Yes, Jamin."

Jamin adjusted his package and lowered himself onto the seat next to her. Jamin turned the stool around to face her. He rotated her seat to face him and positioned his legs to cage her legs between them. He cleared his throat. "Umm, can we talk about what just happened?"

"No, we can't." Shayla's tone and expression were equally blank.

His forehead creased. Understandably, she was upset. If she would allow him to explain things. Jamin appealed, "Shayla, baby, I swear that wasn't what it looked—"

"First of all, you don't have ice cream. And to be more specific, you don't have Ben & Jerry's chocolate fudge brownie or Häagen-Dazs rocky road ice cream. That's a problem. 'Cause I need it when I'm agitated. Second, you promised me stir fry that's the best on this side of Atlanta. I'm starting to get hangry. And drinking on an empty stomach isn't a good look, Jamin. So, now that you've, umm, taken out the trash, can I please have my dinner, Chef-Boyard-Jay?"

His face split into a full grin. He leaned forward, cupped her face in his hands, nibbled on her bottom lip, and then sucked it into his mouth. She tasted like a mixture of apricot and peach from the wine she'd been drinking. Jamin would never get tired of being intoxicated by her exquisite flavor. He hesitantly drew back from the passionate kiss but remained close and murmured on her lips. "How 'bout I put in an Instacart for both of 'em right now? How's two pints of each?"

With a giggle, Shayla nibbled on his bottom lip and nodded. "Uh huh, but I need to eat some food now. My stomach is hitting my back."

"Oh, I'mma feed you baby, but first we need to change the code."

"The code? To what?"

"My house, so the trash doesn't get in like she did tonight. That was my fault. I told you, you've been a distraction. I haven't been thinking. You've been the only thing on the dome, Shayla. I wasn't thinking about changing it. Now we need to. So, what we doing? Gimme some numbers and I'll add it with mine."

She leaned back and furrowed her brows. "Wait. Umm, I'm ... you sure you want me to have it?"

Jamin hung his head. He knew it might be too soon to say it, but his heart was hers. There was nothing to question. He felt her playing in his locs. It was something he loved for Shayla to do. He gripped the sides of her thighs, giving them a firm squeeze. "Shayla baby, I know this was unexpected. Don't get me wrong, if she didn't come up in here tonight, I wouldn't've been thinking 'bout it. But it happened." He lifted his head. "You're my woman now. I want you to feel safe here. You should be able to come and go as you please without worrying if some other chick gon' come through."

"You mean trash." Shayla threw in.

He chuckled with a shake of the head. "Bottom line is, there ain't shit for me to hide from you. Yes, I want you to have it. A'ight, I need four numbers. And don't gimme MiMi's birthday neither."

She brought her arms across her chest and pouted. "Fine. I guess if you're adding some numbers, we can combine our birthdays. Either the months or days we were born."

"Perfect."

Jamin reprogrammed it in the system and showed Shayla how to access it from the front door. Once it was taken care of, he gathered her in his arms, smothering her with kisses. Shayla playfully pushed him away with the reminder he needed to feed her. He pushed himself up while grumbling under his breath. She covered her mouth, giggling.

"What's so funny?"

She pointed to the front of his basketball shorts. Jamin shrugged and gripped his shaft. "What do you expect when you in here with them sexy ass lips? He loves to see your lip gloss poppin' too." He leaned in, giving her another quick peck before putting in the order for her ice cream. Once he placed it, he went over to the sink and washed his hands.

They settled into a light conversation while he continued to prepare dinner. Shayla asked where he learned to cook as Jamin maneuvered between searing the flank steak and starting up the range under the carbon steel wok. He added in some oil and looked up, beaming. "My pops is the chef in our house. Mom is spoiled too. Don't get me wrong. She can do her thing, but I don't think I've ever seen her really throw down the way my pops do. He showed me everything."

"So, what you're saying is that I have my own personal salt bae?"

Jamin threw his head back and laughed. "How did I know your ass was gonna go there?"

"Lemme see you do it."

"Get the fuck outta here."

"Come on, babe, just one time for me. Pleeeease." She begged, poking her lips out.

Jamin shook his head but picked up the salt grinder. For his sexy woman with the luscious lips, he ground out some salt. He took a pinch of it, lifted his arm, and with the flick of his wrist, sprinkled it over the veggies.

She smiled big and clapped. "Thank you!"

"Now come over here and give your salt bae some sugar."

"Gladly. You deserve it." She hopped up from the stool.

Jamin wrapped her into a tight embrace before giving her a quick kiss. "All right, get back over there. All you do is distract me, woman."

Shayla stuck her butt out and teased, "But you like it."

"I sure do. Now get!" Jamin slapped her backside as she sashayed away.

He'd seen his father cook and attentively cater to his mother. They even played with one another the same way. He smiled as he envisioned Shayla and him cultivating a similar relationship. While her attention was drawn to Instagram, Jamin returned to stir-frying the steak and vegetables. He'd just finished putting the rice in the pressure cooker when the doorbell rang. Jamin checked his phone.

"Shayla baby, it's your cousin and Jace. The Instacart delivery is out there too. Can you get it? I gotta finish up here."

"Yep, be right back." She hopped down from the bar stool with a happy squeal.

A few moments later, she returned with the grocery bag of her favorite frozen treats and the loudest pair from their crew on her heels. Jace had his arm draped around Lennie, who was visibly drunk.

She waved with praises, "Jamin, your house is niiiiice!"

"Thanks." He turned around from pulling the plates out of the cabinet.

Shayla put the four cartons in the freezer before rushing over to give him a kiss to express her appreciation. Then, she moved back to the island counter and took her seat.

"What's good, Jay? I see everything's still intact. No furniture's been moved around." Jace said as he came over to the island. He pulled out a chair for Lennie. Once she sat down, he went to the refrigerator to grab them bottles of water. Jace opened the bottle and watched to ensure she drank it.

"I'mma drink it," Lennie shooed him away.

"You better. I need your ass hydrated."

Jamin exchanged a knowing glance with Shayla. She grinned in agreement. It was obvious Lennie and Jace had more brewing between them, even though neither would acknowledge to being in a relationship. Jamin turned off the range and scoffed, "What you mean? Wasn't no furniture gonna be moved around in here. For what and for why?"

Jace rest his elbows on the island and laughed. "Your girl Kels, man. Don't act like you don't know how she is. I figured she would've came up in here wildin'. What happened?"

Jamin rolled his eyes. "She ain't my girl. Don't be disrespectful, nigga. You know my girl right here."

"My bad, Shayla." Jace nodded in her direction. Then he addressed Jamin. "A'ight, what happened?"

Lennie blurted out, "Hey! Where's the food? It smells good in here and I'm hungry."

Shayla laughed, giving herself the facepalm.

Jamin was at the drawer getting the silverware. He chuckled. "I got you. The rice should be finished in—"

A sound from the pressure cooker chimed.

"And there it is. Right on time."

"Need me to help you with anything?" Shayla asked.

"Nah baby, you just sit over there and keep looking sexy. I got this."

"Awww, look at y'all. So stinking cute!"

Shayla groaned, "Hush and drink your water, Lennie."

"I'm just saying y'all are. And you hush." She sassed before taking a swig from the bottle. Lennie set the bottle down and quizzed. "So, are you ready for Vegas?"

Shayla nodded her head enthusiastically. "Definitely, since I've never been. I'm ready to see what Sin City is about."

Jace chimed in. "There's a lot to do. Even with all the time we'll be there, I doubt you'll scrape the surface."

"We've got two weeks. I'm making my list."

"And Jay knows a lot of spots."

"You do, babe?"

Jamin dipped his head in acknowledgement while he continued getting everything prepared for them. "Yep, but go 'head and make your list. Whatever you wanna do, we gonna do. Anything else I can think of that you miss that I think you might like, I'll make sure to add to it."

"I'll give you a few of the activities I've done, too." Lennie offered.

Shayla clapped. "Thank you! I can't wait!"

A few minutes later, Jamin had laid out the dishes - plates, utensils, and serving bowls containing steaming hot rice, sautéed beef, and vegetables - in the middle of the kitchen island. He sat next to Shayla. Jace and Lennie were on the opposite side of the island. Once Jamin said grace over their food, they all dug in.

"Oh, my goodness Jamin! This is delicious!" Lennie announced.

Jace complimented with a mouth full of food. "Ain't nothing new. My boy always puts it down in the kitchen."

Shayla moaned and danced in her seat after the first bite. "Oh-emmm-geee! Mmhmm, babe, this is soooo good!"

He leaned over and warned in a low growl. "Shayla baby, what did I tell you about the moaning? I have no problem leaving them down here and handling this boner you're giving me."

Her cheeks turned red. She whispered, "Sorry, I can't help myself. It's really, really good though. Have you tasted it?"

Jamin chuckled, adjusting himself before focusing on his plate. To prevent ruining his appetite, he only tasted a tiny portion while cooking. It was to ensure he seasoned the food right. He finally savored his first bite of the meal. His mouth literally had a foodgasm. He enjoyed the fusion of spices and herbs dancing on his tongue. The sticky rice was perfect because of the pressure cooker, and the vegetables were sautéed to the right crunch. He cast a glimpse at his woman and friends as they finished up. Their faces said it all. Cooking for people was something Jamin always loved and felt satisfied doing.

Lennie leaned in with her fork raised. "Okay, now you can tell us what happened when your ex busted up in here."

His eyes went to Shayla, who had the wine bottle replenishing her glass.

"Oooh, Shay Bae, pour me one."

"Your ass don't need nothing else to drink 'cept that water." Jace pointed to the bottle in front of her.

Lennie wagged a finger at each of them. "You hush. You pour. And you, tell us what happened."

Shayla got up from the island. Jamin watched her go to the cabinet to grab Lennie a glass and then over to the wine fridge for another bottle.

"I love this for my cousin. You can't take your eyes off her, can you? But go 'head. We're waiting," Lennie urged.

Jace nudged her with his elbow.

"What? We are. You said that bitch was gonna run up on my cousin. Don't look like she did shit. And you already asked so, I'm just following up."

He waited for Shayla to finish pouring Lennie's glass and take her seat. Jamin leaned forward. "First of all, Kels wasn't gon' run up in here and do shit. Secondly, she was outta pocket for coming here without an invite. I handled it and told her ass to bounce. That's it." After taking a sip from his glass and leaning back, Jamin heard Shayla mumble under her breath. He lifted a brow. His eyes shifted to her. "I'm sorry. Did I miss something, baby?"

She spoke directly to Lennie. "This trashy ho' had the code to get in. She came up in here with a peek-a-boo dress that was damn near up her ass. Got all up in my face talking 'bout they had three years' worth of history."

"What?" Lennie shrieked while refilling her glass. Jace took the bottle from her before she overfilled it.

"I told her I knew about *her* history. She got mad when I called her Kels. I was like whatever. Then she said do you think he really wants you?"

"Say what now?"

"I said *think*, I already know he got what he wants. *Me!*" Shayla snorted.

Lennie cheered, "Boom! I know that's right! Bottoms up!"

Shayla clinked her glass against Lennie's when she held it up. Jace laughed. Jamin rocked his head back and forth. He picked up the bottle and poured himself another glass. Shayla tapped her glass for him to refill hers too.

"Me too, Jamin!"

Jace threw up the signal to cut her off. "Hey, Jay man don't—"

"Don't what? I'm grown and can handle my liquor. Well, this is wine. Pour Jamin." Lennie held the glass out and waited until he filled it. She playfully rolled her eyes at Jace. "Thank you, Jamin. You can go 'head, Shay."

Shayla took a big gulp and continued. "And then the trashy ho' had the nerve to say it won't be long if she has anything to do with it. So, I said well, y'all have history, but we're together now. I'm his future. Kels got big mad and said, like hell I am. So, I told her I ain't going nowhere. What are you gonna do about it? That's when Jamin came in."

Jace eyed him. If he hadn't made it downstairs when he did, Jamin wasn't sure what would've happened. Perhaps furniture would've been moved. He finally spoke. "Look, I wasn't about to let them fight. For what?"

"If you did, trust Shay Bae would've molly wop'd her ass in here. Don't let that short, sweet girl fool you. Do you even know where we from?" Lennie's neck rotated.

Shayla shouted, "Decatur, where it's greater!"

When the cousins stood up and recited the first two verses from *Knuck if You Buck*, all Jamin and Jace could do was laugh. He pulled Shayla onto his lap. She threw her arms around his neck. He tweaked her nose. "You would've molly wop'd her, huh?"

"If she thought about coming at me over you, yeah."

Jace chimed in, "Listen, Kels ain't nobody. If anything, she was physical therapy for my boy. She's for the streets."

"A'ight, that's it. I'm done talking 'bout it. Matter of fact, it's time for y'all to go."

"Awww man, the party was just getting started," Lennie whined.

Jace flirted, "Aye, Lennie, I heard there's an afterparty at my house. You coming?"

"Hell yeah! Shay Bae, I gotta go, but I'll call you tomorrow." Lennie almost tripped over her own feet, trying to get over to Jace's open arms.

"Come on. Let's walk 'em out." Jamin lifted Shayla from his lap.

On the way to the front door, the cousins sang their goodbye song. Even though Lennie was still drunk, she held the note and sang as well as Shayla.

She hiccupped, "Love you, Shay Bae!"

"Love you more, Lennie Bean."

Jamin waited until Jace backed out of the driveway to close the door. He set the alarm and draped his arm around Shayla, guiding her back toward the kitchen. "Your cousin is a trip."

"No. How about she's a whole fucking journey."

They spent the next half hour cleaning up the kitchen. Jamin was loading the last plate into the dishwasher when Shayla sauntered in. She'd gone to the bathroom a few minutes earlier. Seeing her lips were shining, he gathered her in an embrace. He gave her a peck on the nose, the lips, and then buried his face in her neck. "Thank you for being patient and understanding. You didn't have to be. A lot of girls wouldn't've been."

"I'm not a lot of girls."

Jamin lifted his head. "You're right about that. Come on, I'm ready to get you upstairs."

"Okay, but first, me and Jimmy have a duet."

"Huh?" He frowned.

Shayla squatted, yanking his basketball shorts down. She gripped his semi-hard shaft, peeked up, and batted her lashes. The blood surged to Jamin's dick instantaneously when she gave it a gentle tug. Jamin saw the fascination in her eyes as she watched his veiny organ pulsate, grow longer, and expand wider. She tugged again, producing clear liquid from the tip. She tilted her head back, parted her lips, and extended her tongue to collect the droplet of precum.

Shayla gazed up at him and whispered against the rim of his dick, "Mmhmm, I'm gonna be blowing, humming, and singing in falsettos with Jimmy."

The gloss smeared across his shaft from her pouty lips as she sucked him into her mouth. Shayla made most of his dick disappear until the tip tapped her tonsils. She peered up at him and pushed another inch inside without gagging. She pulled him out with a loud pop. Then she bobbed her head, tapping the back of her throat again. When she came off his dick again, tears seeped out the corners of her eyes and the spit dribble down her chin. Shayla bobbed her head up and down, slurping and gurgling on his dick. Jamin felt the strength fading in his knees. He reached behind and gripped the edge of the counter for support. His eyes rolled back in his head as she stimulated his balls while doing a variety of tricks on his dick. He'd had his dick sucked in many ways, but Shayla had unrivaled oral skills. The exquisite suction from her mouth was too much. His balls began to throb. She was seconds away from suctioning the life force out of him.

He tried to pull her off and grunted, "Shayla baby ... I'm 'bout to—"

The suction around his shaft tightened, her speed increased, and she cradled his balls until he came. Jamin jerked and erupted violently, shooting his seed down her throat as if he were a volcano. Once she drained him of all his cum, he eased his shaft from her mouth. Shayla licked her lips, sitting back on her heels.

It took a few minutes for Jamin to catch his breath. He finally composed himself and helped Shayla from the floor. She squealed when he scooped her up by the ass. Jamin set her on the edge of the island with his body wedged between her thighs. His hands remained on her butt and Shayla draped her arms around his neck. He dropped a quick kiss on her lips. "Damn, you caught me off guard. I wasn't expecting that kinda performance."

"I can always arrange an encore if Jimmy's up for it." Shayla made seductive, flirtatious noises while curling her lower lip into her mouth.

Jamin lowered his gaze. Jimmy, as she now referred to his dick, had swelled and throbbed in response. They were both ready for an encore and much more. He plucked her lip out of her mouth. While brushing the pad of his thumb across their plushness, Jamin leaned in, and whispered against her lips, "Shayla baby, I've fallen in love with what this mouth do ... it can sang, and it can suck."

CHAPTER 17

Warm, golden streams of light poured into the room, causing Shayla to stir. They'd fallen asleep without closing the blinds. She popped one eye open to peek out the window. Her other eye flew open as she adjusted her vision to the serene view coming into focus. The sky appeared to be blanketed in bursts of red, orange, yellow, pink, and purple for miles. With vivid hues at the mountainous peaks, the colors climbed the rugged desert landscape. Shayla had missed the sunrise. Still, she was in awe of this sight. She'd never been to Nevada or the desert before, so it was a treat to witness the beauty of nature in front of her. Shayla turned over.

Jamin groaned and shifted his position, rolling onto his back, but didn't wake up. It was no surprise to Shayla. He wasn't a morning person. Besides, they'd spent most of the night making love until they fell asleep from exhaustion. Shayla propped up on her elbow, carefully hovering over him. He relaxed the strained expression on his face. It was too precious when he frowned. Even though it could have appeared weird, she was driven to watch her sexy grouch while he slept. She wanted to permanently etch each of Jamin's features in her mind.

Four. It was the total number of beauty moles she'd counted on his otherwise blemish free face. Her favorite one was on his right cheek. With an upturned tip, his nose was a combination between a snub and a button. Her attention went to his lips. They weren't dry, even with his mouth partially open. She discovered he mirrored her routine of moisturizing his lips before night. His pillowy kissers were naturally a shade of pink that would make any girl envious she had to wear lipstick to achieve the same color. Shayla leaned in and lightly pressed her lips against them. He didn't move. His breaths remained steady. Jamin had persuaded her to ignore having morning breath if tongues weren't included. She smiled, thinking how she wouldn't have kissed anyone else without having brushed her teeth. He had her doing several things out of the norm.

Her eyes traveled downward. The sheet came up to his waist, leaving his upper torso exposed. Jamin had tattoos covering more than half of his body. Some were small, while others were much larger. There were too many to count. Shayla thought it was hot and badass he sported so much ink. She traced her fingertips along the various designs across his bulging chest, unsure of where some began and the others ended. All of it was a work of art on a sole masterpiece. She lifted the sheet to peek at another beautiful piece of art. Her tongue slithered out. She moistened her lips at the sight of his Adonis belt. Jamin stirred. He gripped his dick and tugged on it. Shayla let the sheet go. She twisted her head in his direction to find a smug expression on his face.

"Is there something you want down there?" he asked, rolling onto his side, and playfully pushing Shayla onto her back. Jamin latched onto the nipple closest to him. He slipped a hand between her thighs. His soft, yet deft fingers spread her slick folds and probed her slippery walls.

"Hmm, shouldn't Jimmy be tired?"

Jamin lifted his head. "That ain't what I asked you."

"But you promised to take me on a tour of Vegas. How can we do that if you're in here beating my pussy up and I'm too sore to move?" Shayla whined, poking her lips out.

He lowered his head and groaned against her nipple. Jamin switched positions, cradling her in the fold of his arm. He pressed a kiss against her forehead. "You're right I did. But I told you we ain't gon' see all of Vegas in one day. It's too much to do."

"I know, but we're gonna be here for a while, right?"

"Yeah."

"So, we can make this our date activity. You could show me everything Vegas has to offer on a weekly basis."

Jamin nodded in agreement. "I think that's something I can manage."

Shayla rolled out of bed, dragging the sheet with her and off him. "Come on. It's almost ten and we still need to get dressed. We only have what, a few days before it's back to work. And—" The sight of his dick bobbing against his stomach had her mouth gaping. "Really?"

"Can't help it, baby. It's that morning wood." Jamin grinned and folded his arms behind his head.

Her gaze lingered on the long, thick, rock-hard pole as she teased. "If you want that handled, I suggest you come join me in this shower."

Shayla dropped the sheet and scurried into the bathroom once Jamin leaped off the bed after her.

Almost an hour later, they were heading downstairs to the Arya Resort & Casino hotel lobby. One of the concierges greeted them on their way out of the Sky Suites' elevator. Shayla waited while Jamin spoke with him to call for a car service. Her eyes surveyed the grounds where thick groves of palm trees separated three large, teardrop-shaped pools. She craned her neck up to check out the futuristic architectural design of the hotel. Mirrored glass windows made up the entire building's exterior. Jamin drew her focus back to the ground when he draped an arm around her shoulders.

Shayla wrapped her arm around his waist. She peered up at him with inquisitive eyes. "Where are we going?"

"It's a spot I always hit up when I'm out here: Tabletop Brunch. Other than my French toast, they have the best in Vegas. I think you're gonna like it."

"Nope. I'm not trying nobody else's. Yours is now the best and my fave."

Jamin smiled and tweaked her nose. "Good answer."

The concierge got their attention for the driver. Jamin helped Shayla into the SUV and slid in beside her. A few minutes later, they were heading away from the strip. Shayla could hardly contain her excitement. She gazed out the window, watching the busy sidewalk filled with people coming and going. By the time they passed the tenth structure, she lost count of the number of hotels and casinos located along the strip. Jamin told her there were more in an area known as the old part of Vegas or Fremont Street. He promised to take her there on another day.

Shayla tried to relax, but her mind was on everything she wanted to do while they were there. She shifted on the seat toward him, gripped his thigh, and began rambling in almost run-on sentences of all she'd been thinking. "Do you gamble? Which tables do you play? How much do you bet? Are you any good? Have you won? And what about the slot machines? Are they rigged? 'Cause I heard you lose a lot before you win and then it's only a little bit. Which casinos should we go to? How do you even know which ones are good to go to?"

Jamin opened his mouth, but she didn't give him a chance to respond. Her eyes widened as the next idea for an activity popped in her mind.

She clapped her hands. "Oooh, can we go to the Hoover Dam? No, how about the Grand Canyon, but by helicopter! Wait, you aren't scared of heights, are you? Oh babe, please say you're not. I hope not because ... wait, what about ziplining? That's not so bad. I hear you can do that here. Isn't there like a bunch of rides at the top of the Stratosphere? I wanna go there too. Can we, babe? Please!"

Jamin took hold of her hands. "Shayla baby, we will but—"

She squealed and pulled a hand from his grasp to point to a sign outside as they drove by. "Oh-emmm-geee! Babe, I almost forgot Lennie told me about the shows! We have to go to a Cirque du Soleil show, please. There's RuPaul's Drag Race, Pen & Teller, and the Jabbawockeez. Babe, have you seen them dance? And Usher! You know he's doing his residency at MGM too! Are we gonna see him?"

Shayla paused to take a breath. It was then she noticed Jamin frowning at her, quizzically. Her cheeks flushed when she heard chuckling from the front seat. She chewed on her bottom lip. "Sorry."

Jamin chuckled along with the driver as he rocked his head back and forth. He grasped her chin and tugged her lip out from her mouth before leaning in and giving her a gentle peck. "You're so damn cute. No need to be sorry, baby. I know you're excited. I told you I'm gonna show you Vegas. Can't do it all today though."

"I know. Everything was just going through my mind."

He gathered her in his arms and squeezed tight. "We're going to do every one of those activities you named except going to see Usher. You know he's on break, right? It's why we're here. He'll be back after we're done with our residency."

She slapped a palm against her forehead. "Oh yeah, duh."

"Relax, baby." Jamin said in a reassuring tone, with another quick kiss to her lips.

Shayla did as she was told and rested her head against his shoulder. For the remainder of the ride to the restaurant, she enjoyed taking in the desert landscape. Meanwhile, Jamin pointed out a few locations where some of the most notable programs, including *Pawn Stars*, *CSI*, and *Sin City Diaries*, were filmed. He had the driver swing by a shop where they recorded a reality show he appeared on. He'd gone to get a botched tattoo transformed into one of the best pieces of art on his arm.

In admiration, she ran fingertips over the outline of the intertwining piano keys and microphone in awe. Not that she hadn't seen the tattoo before. It was her favorite one of them all. She read the words aloud. Shayla whispered, "*No Music, No Life*. I don't think I could live without it. How sad would we be?"

Jamin was looking straight ahead as he responded. "Pitiful. Life would be absolutely meaningless. Music does so much for the soul. It uplifts the spirits, inspires, and helps a lot of people express their emotions." He twisted his head to face her. "And for some, it brings us together."

Their shared language of love and connection was music, which allowed them to communicate deeply intimate feelings. The song they'd written expressed what they now felt for each other. Jamin became laser-focused on her mouth. She could see the hunger in his eyes. Shayla threw her arms around his neck and crushed her lips against his. Their tongues clashed and tangled in a sloppy, yet fervent kiss. His hand moved up to the back of her neck. He drew her in closer. She moaned.

The driver cleared his throat. "Uhh, I'm sorry to interrupt, Mr. Love. But we're here."

Shayla felt the groan vibrating from Jamin's throat. He eased from their kiss but remained inches from her face. His forehead rested against hers. He gave her a few more pecks before sliding away to reach for the door. Jamin unfastened his seat belt and climbed out. Shayla avoided making eye contact with the driver. She focused on getting her seat belt off. When Jamin opened the door, she hopped out.

"You good, baby?" Jamin asked as he guided her onto the sidewalk.

She smoothed down her top before glancing back. Shayla leaned in and whispered, "Yes, but we got hot and heavy back there with the driver."

Jamin laughed.

"You laughing, but I know he was listening."

"So what? His job is to drive. If he wants to get an earful of what I'm doing to my lady, that's on him. Now come on so I can feed you."

As Jamin promised, brunch was delicious. Shayla decided to get the eggs benedict entrée rather than French toast. She meant what she'd told him. Ever since tasting his, she didn't want to try anybody else's. After they left brunch, Jamin surprised her by taking on a tour of the Hoover Dam.

Shayla's eyes grew wide as he helped her exit the SUV. She bounced on her toes. "Babe! We're really gonna go over this bridge?"

"Babe! You really wanted to go over this bridge!" he mocked.

She playfully punched him in the arm. "Jamin!"

"You got me to get this man to drive us here. Hell yeah, we going. Come on. We gotta get in there now before they start the next tour. It'll give us a few hours to walk this food off."

Their tour was interesting, with a knowledgeable and entertaining guide who happened to be a huge fan of LMK. Over two hours later, Shayla learned a lot about old Las Vegas, Boulder City, Lake Mead and Hoover Dam. She made sure to get Jamin to leave tickets for their tour guide at will call for their concert.

They were settled back in the truck when Shayla probed. "Where are we going now?"

"We're going to participate in another fun activity. Something I've done a couple of times with Jace and 'nem. I think you'll like it. We have about an hour's ride from here."

Shayla took the hint and rested her head against his shoulder. The filling breakfast along with the walk had taken its toll on her. It didn't take long before she dozed off. She woke up to Jamin's soft kisses.

"Time to get up, sleeping beauty. We're here."

Shayla rubbed her eyes. She peeked out the window but couldn't tell where they were. There was a large, commercial building in front of them in addition to an unending horizon of the desert. She questioned him in a whining voice. "Jamin, where are we?"

"Lemme show you."

First, Jamin guided her to the restroom, where she could relieve herself and freshen up. Afterwards, he told Shayla they were at a shooting range for the ultimate outdoor machine gun adventure. Then, he explained they would be going out to a designated area a few miles away, where she would be able to shoot a variety of machine guns, pistols, and rifles.

"Where!" she exclaimed, taking off without any clue of which direction to go.

Jamin tugged her arm, pulling her back to him. "Whoa, baby, hang on. We've gotta sign some paperwork first."

"Well, where is the office? Down there? Let's go. I'm ready to shoot 'em up bang bang, baby!"

He laughed and guided her in the direction of the office. Once they finished filling out the necessary forms, their instructor drove them out to the live gun range. Jamin helped Shayla with getting the earmuffs on. Meanwhile, the instructor set up the assortment of weapons, which included a handgun, a sniper rifle, a belt-fed machine gun, and a submachine gun. They spent the next couple of hours shooting all of them. When she used the .50 cal machine gun and didn't miss the target, Shayla was over the moon. Being a first-time shooter, for her, it was both an exhilarating and terrifying experience.

"Something told me you were gonna get the hang of this," Jamin said as they made their way to the parking lot where the driver waited.

Shayla giggled and boasted. "Well, I am a fast learner."

By the time they reached it, the driver had already opened the back door for them. Jamin gestured with an upward nod. Shayla watched the short, stout man tilt his head in understanding and walk away.

"Sooo, what else you got planned for us?" She inquired, giving Jamin's arm a tight squeeze.

Before helping her inside, he whispered in her ear, "First, I'mma do you. Then we're gonna have dinner and afterwards, I'mma have you for dessert."

Jamin turned the handles to the off position for the jet sprays to stop flowing. The shower was what he needed to get the dirt of the Nevada desert off his body. They'd returned from the outdoor shooting range over an hour ago. If it weren't for Jace and then Derrik calling, he would've joined Shayla when she showered earlier. He grabbed up a plush towel from the rack. A smile tugged at the corners of his mouth. Jamin reflected on the day as he dried off. Shayla thoroughly enjoyed the activities he planned. He looked forward to exploring the rest of Las Vegas with her in the coming weeks. However, he was supposed to be doing her at that precise moment.

Jamin wrapped the towel around his waist and stepped into his shower slides. He emerged from the bathroom to hear her angelic voice singing. Instead of walking into the room and interrupting her, he stopped, resting his shoulder on the door jamb. She sat on the king size bed with her back to him. It wasn't the first time he'd walked in on Shayla belting out a tune. In the past month and a half, since they began dating exclusively, she would sing various songs whenever the mood hit her. Jamin's brows shot up once the lyrics of the song resonated with him.

The towel she had draped around her body fell to her waist. He watched Shayla moisturize her breasts and toffee-colored arms. Lifting her legs up onto the bed to grease them, she continued into the second verse of Tweet's, *Oops (Oh My)*. Shayla scooped the cream into her hand and stood up. Jamin's shaft began to thicken seeing her plump backside. It twitched when she massaged the body butter into her cheeks. The moment she bent over, he pushed himself off the door frame.

Jamin approached her from behind and snaked an arm around her waist. Inhaling the sweet, citrusy fragrance of mangoes and coconut, he pressed his nose to the side of her neck. Shayla lifted an arm, wrapping it around his head. She jutted her hips out against his throbbing erection.

He said in a low growl. "Shayla baby, do you need my help while you touch yourself?"

"Mmhmm, yes." She hissed.

Jamin spun Shayla around to face him. He cradled her neck and lowered his mouth to hers. His tongue invaded her warm, moist, minty-fresh mouth. Their tongues intertwined and slicked together. Jamin broke apart from their kiss for a brief second. He bit her bottom lip. Shayla yelped. She lowered her eyes, and with a naughty grin, bit him back. Jamin growled, crushing his lips against hers. He pushed his tongue past the seam of her lips. She began sucking on it hard and moved her hands from around his neck, up to the bun on the top of his head. After unraveling his locs, she ran her magical hands through his thick hair, massaging his scalp. He caressed her perky curved mounds, being gentle at first, and then rough. His thumb and forefinger tweaked both sensitive buds of her nipples. They tightened to sharp peaks between his fingers. Shayla reached between them and tugged at his towel. It fell to the floor. She rubbed her slick folds over his leaking tip. He withdrew from her mouth and took a step back. Her attention went below his waist. She moistened her luscious, swollen lips with a swipe of her tongue. He pinned Shayla with an intent look. She met the heat of his gaze with her own.

Jamin scooped Shayla up with a quick, effortless motion while still making eye contact. He carried her over to the round table that sat by the floor-to-ceiling windows. Jamin placed her in the center and pushed her knees up to her ears, exposing the pink slit between her thighs. He was met with a gushing hello from her pussy. His nostrils flared as the arousing scent from her pussy brought out the primal, animalistic urge. He bowed his head. Running his tongue up the slit, he used it to tease her wet folds open. Shayla shuddered as he slithered inside the meaty, slippery walls. Her exquisite sweetness coated his tongue. Jamin savored the flavor for a moment. Then he attacked her pussy like a ravenous animal, treating her as though she were his prey. Under the assault of his tongue, she squirmed and thrashed her head from side to side. She tried to close her legs, but he restrained her.

"Jaaamin! I'm ... oooh ... I'm about to ..."

Her words were lost. Jamin peeked up to find her unraveling. He released the suction he had on her clit. Spreading the soaked vertical lips, he pushed a long finger inside her. Jamin worked a second finger into her pussy. Latching onto her sweet berry again, Jamin sucked and stroked her G-spot, sending her into a frenzy.

Shayla dug her nails into his shoulders and arched into him, screaming, "Yes! Yes! Oh my god, Jamin! Yesss!"

Jamin slid his hands under her cheeks, slinging Shayla's trembling thighs over his shoulders, he sucked her juices clean off his fingers from knuckle to digit. He grabbed her ass and hoisted her up.

"Wha-wha-what are you doing, Jamin?" Shayla screeched, gripping his shoulders tight.

He responded a low growl, "I'm licking my plate clean."

Jamin slipped his tongue between the drenched fat lips, circled around the hooded button, and inside her hot pink meat. He pinned her back against the window and feasted on her pussy until Shayla quaked with pleasure again. She shook uncontrollably, spewing out more juices. Jamin attempted to lap it all up. Instead, he almost choked. If this was how he was going out, he'd gladly drown in her taste. Chuckling at the thought, Jamin turned his head to burp, and then he commenced to slurping her pussy dry. A scream of pleasure tore from Shayla's lips, and her thighs clamped around his head. He pried them open before she snapped his neck.

Jamin moved over to the table. He eased her down to the center, wrapping her legs around his waist. She reached up to touch his face and dropped her hand fast. She lowered her eyes, and he saw the redness in her cheeks.

"Hey."

Shayla raised her doe-like brown irises to meet his.

"What did I tell you?"

"I know. It still takes some getting used to, is all."

Jamin leaned forward inches from her face. "Wanna taste how sweet you are?"

Shayla tried to lower her head, but Jamin cupped her chin and lifted it, keeping their faces aligned. He watched her with curious intent. She shrugged and then nodded. Her fingers traced his lower lip. Jamin's mouth slanted over hers, landing a punishing kiss. His probing tongue demanded a response. Once Shayla slipped her tongue in between his lips, their tongues aggressively circled each other like two snakes. He could taste a mixture of her arousal and minty mouthwash, both delicious in flavor. Their sloppy kiss lasted for a minute. Jamin finally pulled himself away from her delectable lips. Shayla leaned back, tucking her swollen bottom lip into her mouth.

"You have no idea what that shit does to me."

"What?"

"This." He replied while nibbling and giving pecks. "I ... love it... when you ... bite ... your lip ... like ... this." Shayla moaned. He was teasing her slick entrance with rubbing his swollen tip back and forth across her clit. "And see how hard you make me? Shhhit, Jimmy loves it too."

Shayla inched to the edge of the table, grabbed his shaft, and tried to push him in. He knocked her hand away. "Nah uh, I don't need your help. I got this."

"Jaaamin, come on babe, please."

Her voice sounded like a kid whining for something they wanted and couldn't have. Jamin almost laughed, but wouldn't dare. It was cute and sexy as fuck, seeing her beg for him to make love to her. "Please what?"

"I-I'm gonna ... I wa-wanna ..."

"You want what? Talk to me, Shayla baby."

"Yes, that's it Jamin! That's it!"

"Nah, I wanna hear you say it. Tell me whatchu want?" Jamin slowed his stimulating pats on her clit to an instant stop.

Shayla spoke through labored panting. "Come! I wanna come!"

"And?"

"You! I want you ... and-and Jimmy ... to fuck me! Jamin, pleeeease! Fuck me!"

"Atta girl." Jamin replied with a smirk. He slid his hands under her hips, hooked her legs over his arms, and pushed every inch into her velvet warmth. She parted her lips, but Jamin devoured them, exchanging another sloppy kiss. He bucked hard, pummeling her insides. With every dip, twist, and stroke he delivered, Jamin worked to rearrange her cervix. He knew he'd stretched her pussy to the limit. She gasped with each measured, powerful thrust. Shayla squirmed under him but clung to him, pleading for more. Her voice almost sounded hoarse from screaming out his name. He slowed his strokes in the scalding hotness that clenched him like a vise-grip.

"Don't stop, Jamin! You're gonna make me come so hard."

"I know baby 'cause ... fuck!" He gritted out.

Jamin's hands went to her waist. In a futile attempt to slow down his nut, he withdrew partially, leaving the thick helmet of his shaft lodged inside. Shayla lifted her hips to meet his thrust. He plunged deeper, planting himself to the hilt. She hissed, a sound that was half-pain, half-pleasure when Jamin's length speared her. His dick glided in and out as he pistoned more rapidly. Hard, deep, and aggressive strokes rammed into her. Her velvety slick walls rippled before spasming around his dick.

She cried out, "Jamin!"

"Shayla baby ... arrrrgh!"

The orgasm hit them at the same time. Where their bodies connected, passion exploded in one hot, sticky release, sending both into a shuddering fit of pure heat and pleasure. Jamin held onto Shayla as their breaths mingled and mixed hotly. She rested her head on his shoulder. A few minutes had passed when he heard her release a sigh.

"You good, baby? You need anything?"

Shayla shook her head. "No, I'm okay."

"You just let out that loud ass sigh. Was it a good thing?"

Instead of responding, an impish grin settled on her face.

"What?" Jamin asked with an eyebrow raised.

Shayla pointed towards the window. "Getting my pussy ate and then fucked mindless while watching the sunset behind us. Yeah, Claude Debussy was right, there's nothing more musical than this."

CHAPTER 18

Shayla could hardly contain the smile splitting her face. After a week in Sin City, Jamin surprised her by doing some of the activities from her list. So far, he'd taken her to the Stratosphere Observation deck, the Ferris wheel at the LINQ hotel, and the Bellagio's indoor botanical gardens which included a stop to view its infamous water fountains. Jamin expanded the list by including a few other thrilling things to do and popular restaurants. There was far more to show her, considering they still hadn't made it to Fremont Street. With the first show of their residency happening the following night, he suggested they keep it simple and hang with their crew later that afternoon. She snuck a peek up at Jamin. Her heart could've burst from the genuine feelings overflowing from within.

Shayla felt like pinching herself. The towering, honey-toned African king walking beside her was indeed her man. Jamin glanced down. His lips curled into a smile, revealing the full platinum grill. It was hard not to fawn over him. Her man was fine as hell and rocking the flashy mouthpiece added to his sex appeal. Her lashes fluttered. Shayla bit into her bottom lip.

Jamin held out his hand in front of her and halted in his stride. "Nah uh, come on. Now you know what that shit does to me."

Shayla's brows drew together. Tilting her head up at him, she replied with a sly tinge in her voice. "Babe, what are you talking about?"

Jamin dragged his thumb across her bottom lip. He leaned closer, putting an arm around her waist. His breath tickled her ear as he growled. "Shayla baby, you don't wanna play this game with me. 'Cause I have no problem taking you in one of these bathrooms down here and bending you the fuck over."

She should've known better than to tease him. Jamin didn't play fair. He pressed the thick bulge against her butt. Her core muscles clenched. She grasped his arm tight right as her knees wobbled. A shaky breath escaped her lips. "Jamin."

"Whatchu want, baby?"

"Shayla Childs?"

The hairs stood up on the back of Shayla's neck. She whipped her head in the direction where the voice came from. Shayla stepped away from Jamin. As she shifted on her feet, she saw his confused expression. It was no time to explain. She had to compose herself to face the coconut brown-skinned woman with the waist-length, Brazilian bundles heading toward them. Shayla's eyebrows shot up when she saw the tall, dark man strolling behind her. Instantly, she knew the next few minutes would be cringy.

"I thought that was you!" The woman exclaimed, stopping a few feet away from them. She turned to address her companion, who was now standing right beside her. "Erwin, isn't it ironic we're seeing her?"

He unabashedly gave Shayla a once over and licked his lips. Erwin nodded in agreement. "Yeah, real ironic."

A devious grin crept onto the woman's face. She tossed the fake weave and returned her attention to Shayla. "I swear to God, I was just telling him it would be crazy if we ran into you and look. Here you are, in the flesh. So, Shayla Childs, how are you?"

Before answering, Shayla cast another quick glance at Erwin. His tongue darted out suggestively as he stared back at her. He wet his lips. However, instead of hydrating them, a film of white crusty ash appeared. It took everything for her not to gag. Shayla cut her eyes to the woman and forced a smile. "I'm good."

"*Good?* Heh, no need to be modest, Shayla."

She maintained a poker face and quipped. "Modest? Why, not at all. However, if you need more emphasis, how about I'm better than ever."

The woman's eyes flitted over to Jamin. She checked him out from head to toe and back up, pausing below his waist. She swiped her tongue over her lips, twirling her hair.

I know this thirsty bitch didn't. Shayla cleared her throat.

The woman brought her eyes up and over to meet Shayla's icy glare. A sly smirk formed on her face as she lifted her shoulders. She tossed the fake hair, gestured with a dismissive hand, and snorted. "I bet you are. Now, why don't you introduce us?"

Shayla's ears grew hot. Impulse made her want to connect a fist with the woman's mouth to knock the sneering grin off her face. But Shayla knew the consequences would end up doing more harm than good. Sure, she could knock this bitch the fuck out, but she would end up arrested. Which would likely result in her being unable to perform the following night. Shayla chose to exercise restraint. She didn't bother masking the dullness in her voice. "Jamin, this is Akeela or I think it's Ameeka … and umm err Dwight—"

'The woman kissed her teeth and rotated her neck when she corrected. "It's *Aneeka Skyy* and *Erwin Davies.*"

Whatever. Better be glad I didn't say Dwight around his lips. Shayla deadpanned. "Yeah, right what you just said. Well, I'm sure y'all already know this is Jamin Love."

"Such a pleasure to meet you, *Jamin.*" Aneeka drawled out, proffering a hand to him.

To avoid slapping the stiletto nails out of her man's face, Shayla shoved her hands into the pockets of her jeans. She narrowed her eyes at Jamin, but relaxed when he gave her a subtle head shake. Shayla knew better. She had nothing to be jealous of. Jamin would never disrespect her by entertaining a woman openly flirting with him. His handshake with Aneeka was brief. Afterwards, he turned to Erwin and the two men tipped their heads, acknowledging each other. The awkward pause which followed was unavoidable. Shayla didn't have anything to say. What could she say? This was an unexpected and an unwanted reunion.

The silence was broken by Aneeka. "Well, I must say this is so cool. Us running into you. It's been what almost four years?"

"Yeah, probably. Who's keeping count?"

"Well, it's a shame that we haven't kept in touch all these years." Aneeka criticized.

Shayla kept a poker-faced expression. Aneeka was putting on a show, but she didn't know for whom. It wasn't necessary to be phony. They were, at best, acquaintances.

"Far too long," Erwin added before Shayla could respond. Drool oozed at the corner of his mouth. Using his thumb and forefinger, Erwin swiped away the saliva. He folded his lips in his mouth, staring at her.

Ewww. She had to look away to avoid gagging. Shayla couldn't believe his ugly ass was flirting with her. She didn't miss the disgusted expression on Aneeka's face as she rolled her eyes at him too. Out the corner of her eye she saw Jamin mean-mugging Erwin. It was time to wrap up this blast from her past. Shayla gave his arm a gentle tug. "Yeah, it was cool running into y'all, but we've gotta go. Right, babe?"

"I know you ain't trying to run off." Aneeka griped as she folded her arms across her chest. Then she held up her hand. "You know what, on second thought. This is what you're used to doing. Running away, that is."

Oh, this bitch is trying it. Shayla took in a sharp breath. After releasing the oxygen, she spoke in an even tone. "Ain't nobody running away. We already have plans. Now if you will, excuse us."

"Oh wow, I see you're doing breathing exercises. Are we still struggling with anxiety? Hmm, how's it working for you? I have heard it's better to woosah it out."

She'd heard enough. Shayla tapped Jamin's arm. "Yeah, it is especially when you're about to lose your cool. We've got to go. See ya round."

"Night." Jamin said with an upward nod. He then placed his hand in the small of Shayla's back and guided them away from the pair.

"Hey." Aneeka called out to them.

Shayla stopped. She glanced up at Jamin. They both twisted their heads to look back at her.

"We're gonna come and see you perform."

"Okay." Shayla mumbled and turned to walk away. They'd barely taken a few steps before she felt someone grab her arm. Breaking away, she whirled around.

Aneeka held her hands up as a sign of surrender.

"What?" Shayla said in a huff. As Aneeka moved to stand next to her and leaned in, Shayla lowered her eyes. Aneeka's voice was low, where only Shayla could hear.

"I hope you don't croak. But if you do, this time don't run. Just suck it up." Aneeka retreated a few paces, revealing a sinister grin.

Shayla was not about to let Aneeka get under her skin. She looked her up and down. Taking the steps to close the distance between them, Shayla scoffed, "You don't need to hope for anything. And I sure as hell don't need your advice. Don't worry Akeela, I got this." Shayla turned on her heel, grabbed Jamin's hand, and stormed off.

"Ugh, it's Aneeka!"

Shayla didn't bother turning around to acknowledge her. They were down the hall and approaching the double doors of the bowling alley when Jamin finally asked.

"You good, baby?"

She peeked back. She lost sight of Aneeka, her fake weave, and Erwin in the crowd. Rolling her eyes, Shayla mumbled, "I'm fine."

"Nah, I can tell you not. Who were they?" Jamin asked with a tone full of concern. Instead of opening the doors to the bowling alley, he led her off to the side.

Her back was against the wall, literally. Shayla lifted her eyes to Jamin's curious yet comforting gaze. She didn't want to talk about them, but he wasn't about to let it go. Blowing the air out of her cheeks, Shayla shared Aneeka and Erwin were the unpleasant reminders of that disastrous day in New York. "Of all people, those two were still back there when I ran off the stage. I collided with Akeela, almost knocking her over and tripping myself up in the process." Shayla looked away. Her thoughts drifted back to that exact moment in time. She hugged herself, rubbing her forearms. Her face contorted into a frown. The vivid memory of Erwin catching her before she could fall flashed before her eyes. She shivered at the way he groped her. "Ugh, and that creep, Erwin, got in a few cheap feels on my ass. He caught me before I fell."

Jamin's brows shot up and then they knitted together. He stalked off, heading down the hall toward the casino.

Shayla tugged him back in her direction. "Jamin, they're long gone by now.

He continued to scan the crowd of people.

"Babe, can you look at me?" Shayla pleaded.

Jamin mumbled something inaudible under his breath. Shayla reached up and cupped his face. She guided him in, lowering his head. "Hey." She waited for him to focus his eyes on hers. "Babe, listen to me. That was years ago, okay? As much as I wanted to bust Akeela's ass in the mouth for half of the slick shit she said, she wasn't worth going to jail for. Neither is Erwin. Okay?"

He nodded. Jamin took hold of her wrists before leaning in and kissing her. "You're right. I'm sorry. Just knowing that ashy nigga had his hands on you … my bad, baby. Go 'head and finish."

Shayla sighed, "So anyway, Akeela's nosey ass asked where I was running off to right as the show producers made it back there. They asked the same question. Just like I froze on stage, there I was backstage with all eyes on me again and, and I couldn't …" She paused and took in a deep breath. After a silent count to ten, Shayla exhaled slowly. Her breathing remained steady, but the pace of her heart quickened. Inside, everything trembled. Reliving that moment brought on the anxiety episodes. She needed to relax. She had to.

Once more, Shayla breathed in through her nose, allowing oxygen to fill her lungs, and then exhaled all the air out of her mouth. "I couldn't handle their stares either. You know the rest. I bounced and didn't look back. So, Akeela got what she wanted. I was out of the competition, but the joke was on her. Tréy Legend won. Anyway, I hadn't seen them since. Nobody from back then really. Wasn't close to nobody and thank God I didn't have a social media account for them to drag me for filth. Of course, it would be my luck to run into those two assholes today."

Jamin wrapped an arm around her waist and pulled her close. "I know if we see that motherfucka again, I'mma knock *Dwight from 'round his lips* out."

"See, you're just as bad as me. I knew you would've caught that when I messed up his name."

"Yeah, I heard you. His ashy ass was drooling all over my baby. What he needs is some ChapStick."

"That or a vat of chicken grease." Shayla laughed.

Jamin laughed, planting a kiss on her lips. He stepped back. "And your ass is wild for calling that girl Akeela. You know that's not her name."

"Whatever it is, it ain't worth me trying to remember."

"True. Well, come on. We gotta get inside. I know they probably got the lanes set up already."

He guided Shayla through the doors of Las Vegas Bowl. They went up the escalator to the second floor of the establishment with an industrial interior design. Shayla was in awe of the open ceiling containing exposed pipes, ducts, and the surrounding brickwork. There was a large disco ball which hung from the ceiling. It was cosmic bowling, so patterns of laser and disco lights illuminated the hardwood floors. The combined noise from the heart pounding music, bowling balls hitting the lanes and pins almost drowned out Jamin's voice when he called her name.

Shayla leaned in. "I didn't hear you, babe. Say what?"

"We gotta get shoes. I'mma need your size."

While Jamin went to the counter to take care of getting their shoes, Shayla excused herself to the restroom. Truthfully, she needed a moment of reprieve. She had to get her head together. Running into Aneeka and Erwin had left her rattled. She wished they hadn't seen her. For them to speak and keep it moving would've been asking for too much. Aneeka was being petty. She knew full well, they never shared more than a brief greeting in passing during those months leading up to the final competition. Shayla wondered how different things might've been had she stayed.

"Don't croak. And if you do, this time don't run. Just suck it up."

"Excuse me? Mind if I get a paper towel?" A voice interrupted her thoughts.

Shayla looked up from the sink. "Oh yes, of course. Let me get out of your way."

After exiting the restroom, she saw Jamin waiting outside with their bowling shoes. Shayla followed him on the far end of the bowling alley to the last two lanes. The dimly lit area had two large leather sofas facing the other with a long wooden coffee table separating them. There was also a matching ottoman, which sat on one end of the coffee table. Lennie was standing over Daria, who was seated at the bowling machine inputting names on the scoreboard. Zayne and Jace were over at the ball rack. From what Shayla could tell, Zayne was helping Jace pull his fingers out of a ball.

"How the hell you managed to do that, nigga? You ain't see them holes was too small for your fat fingers?" Jamin teased, making his way over to them.

Jace shot back. "If you ain't gon' help, don't bring your ass over here."

Shayla greeted her cousin Lennie, who had her arms open wide. After speaking to Daria, Shayla sat on the ottoman to change into her bowling shoes. By the time she finished tying them, a server came over to get everyone's order. She needed a couple of shots to calm her nerves and made sure to order them.

"Let's get this game going. I'm ready to bust some ass out here." Jace bellowed, approaching one of the lanes.

Jamin finished tying his shoe and looked up, taunting him. "Nigga, you couldn't even get the right ball. How you gon' bust somebody's ass?"

"I got the right one now. That's all that matters. And nigga, we on the same team, so shut up. Now Daria, I don't wanna hear shit about it ain't fair either. Rack 'em up. Let's go!"

Lennie stepped up to the other lane, since her name was up first. The two playfully argued about who should go first. Finally, Jace stepped back with his hand stretched out. "My daddy taught me better, Lennie. Ladies first."

Daria came and sat next to Shayla. She watched as her cousin nodded at Jace. Lennie took a few steps and threw the ball. Next thing Shayla heard was the ball hitting the lane with a loud thwap and seconds later a crack. Her eyes grew big as saucers as the ten pins fell, flew, and spun in different directions. She and Daria hopped up to meet Lennie with hi-fives and congratulatory praises for hitting a strike right out the door.

"Yeah, now top that!" Lennie boasted as she strutted past Jace.

Jace shot back. "Beginner's luck. Watch a pro and this curve, girl."

The friends erupted in laughter a minute later when his curve ball turned right into the gutter. He turned with his face twisted up in a frown. He opened his mouth.

Lennie threw up a hand and pointed to the lane. "Nah, we don't wanna hear it. Let's see if you can pick up that spare."

Shayla saw the server had also returned with their drinks and appetizers. While Jace focused on his second attempt, Shayla knocked back one of her shots. Watching his ball travel down the lane, her mind replayed Aneeka's words: *"Don't croak. And if you do, this time don't run. Just suck it up."*

His ball curved again. Instead of going into the gutter, he managed to pick up four pins. The next words came as a taunt to her psyche: *At least he tried without running away.*

Shayla threw back her second shot and closed her eyes for a moment. She needed to stop worrying. Nothing was going to happen. History would never be so cruel as to repeat itself. Jamin, who was seated across from her, was looking at her when she opened her eyes. He winked and flashed her a platinum smile. Shayla's cheeks warmed. Her stomach fluttered as though it was full of butterflies. His smile always seemed to have that effect on her. For the moment, her thoughts were easily occupied with her sexy man's face.

"Better luck next time," Lennie called out to him as Jace walked away, rocking his head from side to side. He flipped her the middle finger.

"Don't be a sore loser," Daria teased on her way up to the lane.

She knocked down half of her pins and picked up the spare. Zayne, like Jace, only managed to knock down four pins between his two turns. When it was Shayla and Jamin's turn, the competitiveness kicked in. Shayla was happy she picked up her spare. Jamin, on the other hand, like his teammates, didn't fare any better. He scored five with his first attempt and then rolled a gutter ball with the second turn. They thought they would do better with some food and drinks, but for most of the frames, the girls maintained hitting strikes and picking up spares. They were well into their second game, on the tenth and final frame when Shayla thought she saw a couple who looked like Aneeka and Erwin.

There was no way she could miss that weave. Those Brazilian bundles were cheap and sat on top of Aneeka's head like a nest. Erwin was as tall as Jamin, so she couldn't overlook his crusty ass either. Shayla scanned the crowd of people hanging out in the spacious lounge area. She fixed her eyes on the couple. Her heart thumped out of her chest. She held her breath. The woman turned her head to look right at her.

"Shayla baby, it's your turn!"

She whipped her head toward Jamin while clutching her chest. Suddenly Shayla felt lightheaded. She needed to be sure it wasn't them. Shayla twisted her head and her eyes flitted back in the direction of the lounge.

"Don't croak. And if you do, this time don't run. Just suck it up."

The woman she thought was Aneeka wasn't. The man standing next to her wasn't Erwin. She let out the ragged breath that she'd been holding. Shayla refocused her attention, meeting Jamin's puzzled yet concerned expression. The humming in her ears seemed to drown out the sounds of everything around her. The surrounding noises of the bowling balls hitting the lanes, pins falling, and her friends' laughter were muffled. She repeated the exercise of inhaling and exhaling. Shayla felt Jamin's strong arm around her waist.

"Hey, hey look at me."

Her eyes drifted up to meet his. She forced a weak smile. "Hey babe."

"You good?" Jamin asked as he traced small circles on her lower back.

Shayla pressed her forehead against his chest and inhaled deep. She was able to relax her nerves some by inhaling her man's intoxicating woodsy scent. He smelled so fucking good. She couldn't resist wetting her lips. Releasing a deep breath, she murmured, "Mmhmm yeah, but I might've had a bit too much to drink. After this game I think I should go lie down. I'm starting to feel a little tired anyway."

"Aye, do y'all wanna finish this game or go back to your room with all of that?" Jace called out to them.

Jamin lifted a hand, giving him a middle finger. He grinned, and that did it for her. Shayla grabbed his face, giving him a kiss that elicited a groan from their friends. For the sake of their grumbling, they kept it short. She eased out of Jamin's arms and went over to the lane. After the first attempt, she left two pins standing. She finished her game with picking up the spare.

"Hells yeah, that's what I'm talking about! In yo' face, Jace! Now who's the loser?" Lennie danced around and taunted him.

He sucked his teeth. "Whatever. I still say that was all beginner's luck. Let me see y'all do it again."

Shayla shook her head, rejecting the challenge. "Sorry to be a party pooper, y'all, but I'm feeling all those drinks. I need to take it down."

"You're not alone. Count me out too. I have an appointment with the masseuse first thing in the morning. And I refuse to hurt my fingers and arm trying to prove how sorry you are at yet another activity." Daria mocked Jace while untying her bowling shoes.

Zayne and Jamin laughed as they joined them on the sofas to remove their shoes. They gave the girls their props on winning. Whereas Jace complained and even accused them of cheating. He and Lennie argued about it on the way up to the desk to return their shoes.

"How you figure is what I wanna know?" Lennie yelled after Jace.

Jace shrugged. "Ion know, but trust me, I know y'all asses cheated somehow."

Shayla tugged on Jamin to lean in. She whispered, "I guess we know who's the sore loser in the crew."

"Since we were kids. And I'm not trying to be out all night with him, trying to prove a point that he's not one. He wants to shoot some pool. So, me and Zee gonna have to let his ass win a couple games to smooth out this loss." Jamin gathered her into an embrace and shared a quick kiss. "I ain't trying to stay out long. See you a little while."

After the guys left them, Shayla, Lennie, and Daria walked outside for the rideshare to take them back to their hotel. While the trio waited, they took a few selfies in front of the bowling alley boasting of their win. To be funny, Lennie decided to post the pics on IG and tag the guys. Within seconds, Jace commented on each of them with angry emojis calling them cheaters.

They were seated in the back of the rideshare a little while later when Shayla giggled and asked Lennie. "Should we tell them we used to play in a league?"

"Hell no! Next time we're runnin' them pockets since Jace got all that mouth. We're gonna pull out the Hammers and show them what we're really working with. You think he's mad now? He's gonna be big mad for days … maybe weeks. Hmm, I think I need a new Birkin."

Daria turned around in the passenger seat with her mouth open, and then she smirked. "Y'all are dirty, but please teach me."

"You know we got you, girl!" Lennie said, exchanging a high-five.

The entire ride to the hotel, the trio discussed how and when they would get together to practice with Daria. They would have to wait until the group had a break between shows before they could challenge the guys for a rematch. Their practice would start in another week once Lennie could come back to visit.

"I can't wait! All right, I'll see y'all tomorrow!" Daria waved from her room as the elevator doors closed.

The cousins shared another good laugh about the night's win. When the doors of the elevator opened, Lennie and Shayla sang their song and hugged each other before parting ways. Lennie's room was on the opposite end of the hall. Shayla waited for Lennie to open her door and step inside before entering hers.

She stepped across the threshold, closed the door, and pressed her back against it. The night had ended with some much-needed laughter. However, being alone her thoughts were once again consumed with stress about a scenario that might not happen. She hated crossing paths with Aneeka. That petty heffa succeeded in planting a seed of doubt. It'd sprouted out of control in a matter of hours. Now Shayla wasn't so sure history wouldn't repeat itself. *What if it does happen again? What if I can't recover from this? What if I totally screw this up?* Suddenly, the air in the room became too dense to breathe. The pace of her heart quickened.

Shayla rummaged through her bag to find her phone. She swiped across the screen to Jamin's name, but hesitated. Instead of sending the call, she scrolled to Lennie's name. Again, she paused. Her thumb hovered over her cousin's name. Shayla couldn't send the call. Her fight-or-flight instinct kicked in and she felt compelled to leave the room.

With a shaky breath, Shayla whispered to herself. "Relax. It's going to be fine. I've got this."

CHAPTER 19

Jamin rolled over with his arm extended. His dick was hard as steel. After hanging out with Jace and Zayne longer than planned, he came in and immediately fell asleep. Now that he was up, or rather his dick was, he wanted to slide deep inside Shayla's honey pot. He touched the space on the bed where she should've been and groaned. *Damn. She must be in the bathroom.* A few minutes passed. Jamin struggled to keep his eyes open. He could feel himself dozing off.

BEEP! BEEP! BEEP!

"Fuck!" Jamin shouted, almost jumping out of the bed.

He scrambled, reaching for the nightstand to get his phone. Finally grabbing it, he disabled the blaring alarm. He squinted and shielded his eyes. It was painfully bright from the sun pouring into the room. Pushing himself off the bed, Jamin trudged over to the window and yanked the cord to close the blind. He noticed Shayla wasn't in bed as he turned around. His first thought was she must've been in the bathroom again, but he didn't hear her singing. He headed there, calling out to her. "Shayla baby, you in the—"

Jamin froze mid-step. His attention was drawn to her side of the bed. It looked as though she hadn't slept there at all. Where the hell is she? He thought to himself, heading back over to the nightstand. Jamin grabbed his phone and called Shayla. It rang until her voicemail picked up. He didn't bother leaving a message. Hanging up, he waited several seconds, and called back. Again, Shayla's voicemail answered. Jamin frowned. He pulled the phone from his ear, ended the call, and keyed in a text message.

> Shayla baby, you good? Where you at? Hit me back when you get this. – **Jamin**

Next, Jamin went to the bathroom to take care of his hygiene. He brushed his teeth and took a quick shower. She wasn't there when he returned to the bedroom. Jamin moisturized his skin, then threw on a tank top and a pair of sweatpants. Afterwards, he checked his phone. There were no missed calls. A scowl formed across his face as he sat on the edge of the bed. Shayla didn't mention she had something to do, nor that she would be going somewhere that morning. He twisted his head to look back at where she should've been sleeping. Last night, they parted ways after the bowling alley so she could get some rest. The only two people she could possibly be with were Lennie or Daria. Jamin decided to contact his friend first.

"Hey Jamin, what's up?" Daria's cheery voice echoed in his ear.

He maintained a steady tone in his voice and inquired. "Hey, 'sup Daria. Uhh by any chance is Shayla with you?"

"No, I just got back from my massage. I was about to see what everybody else was up to. Wanna go to brunch before heading over to MGM?"

Jamin's eyebrows slammed together. He glanced around the room. Everything was exactly how they'd left it before leaving for the bowling alley. She hadn't been in there at all. Something wasn't right. He needed to call Jace.

"Did you hear me?" Daria asked, interrupting his thoughts.

He admitted. "Umm no, I'm sorry. My mind was on something else."

"Everything okay?"

"I hope so."

"What do you mean? What's wrong, Jamin?"

"I'mma hit you back. I need to hit up Jace.

"Is it Shayla? Did something happen, Ja—"

Jamin didn't have time for Daria to drill him about it. He didn't know enough to tell her. All Jamin could think about was the woman he loved wasn't there and, to make matters worse, he had no clue where she was. His eyes widened. The revelation hit him hard. *The woman I love.* He hadn't expressed those words to her yet, but he was madly and deeply in love with Shayla. It was time he told her. The realization that he still didn't know where she was had Jamin's stomach twisted in a knot. Without wasting any more time, he swiped his thumb across the screen.

Jace's voicemail greeting echoed in his ear. Jamin couldn't sit still anymore. He got up from the bed. After sending Jace a text, he tried Shayla's phone again. Like before, it rang without an answer. He hung up when the voicemail picked up and began pacing the length of the room. Then his phone rang. He held his breath hoping it was Shayla. His heart sank as he peeked down at the display.

Jamin didn't bother giving Jace a proper greeting. He needed to know where his girl was. "Hey, is Lennie with you?"

"Nah, I left her a lil' while ago. What's up with the urgent text? I was in the shower when you called. Nigga, I'm surprised your ass is even up after last ni—"

"I can't find Shayla!" Jamin uttered rashly.

"What you mean you can't find her? How the hell you lose her?"

"She wasn't here when I woke up. And she's not answering her phone. I checked with Daria first, but she's not with her. I thought she might've been with Lennie. I didn't want her to panic. That's why I called you."

"Jay, just relax, man. You getting yourself worked up for nothing. Maybe she went downstairs."

Jamin shouted, "Don't tell me to relax! I know she didn't go downstairs. Did you fucking hear me? She wasn't here when I woke up. And from what I can tell, she wasn't here last night."

"But they all left together. And I know Lennie had to come up there with her. She's down the hall from y'all."

"Jace, I'm looking at her side of the bed. She didn't sleep here and trust me. Shayla wouldn't leave without telling me. Something's wrong."

"Okay, okay, let me throw something on. I'll be right up. And I'll call Lennie."

"No! Don't say nothing yet. Just tell her to meet you here. I don't want to alarm her yet, but if we need to …" Jamin hesitated. He didn't want to say it. The seriousness of the situation, however, became clear. Shayla was missing. His voice was thick with emotion. "If we need to call the police. Lemme go. I was supposed to call Daria back."

"Don't worry 'bout Daria. I'll call her and grab Zee on my way. See you in a minute. And Jay, for real, relax. It's not gonna come to that," Jace reassured before ending the call.

Jamin's shoulders slumped, and he hung his head low. He desperately wanted to believe Jace, but a sense of helplessness overcame him. Shayla had never been to Las Vegas before. She didn't know where to go. She wouldn't venture out on her own either. This was out of the norm for her to leave without telling him, so it didn't make sense.

He whispered out loud, "Shayla baby, where are you?"

A few minutes later, there was a knock on the door. Jamin opened it to see Daria standing in the hallway. He stepped aside, allowing her to come in.

"Hey, Jace told me. Still no word from her?" Daria placed a hand on his arm, her voice filled with concern.

Rocking his head from side to side, Jamin mumbled a negative answer. He couldn't meet her eyes. Out of nowhere, a lump formed in his throat. Excusing himself, he quickly headed for the bathroom. Jamin closed his eyes and leaned against the back of the door. He needed a moment to calm down. It was hard to ignore the panic stirring in his spirit. The last time Jamin felt like this was when he lost his cousin Cami. *Not again, God. I can't do this.* His heart couldn't take losing Shayla too. He willed his body from the door and went to the sink. While splashing the cool liquid on his cheeks, Jace's voice carried into the bathroom. He grabbed a hand towel from the rack. Jamin peered up into the mirror. Drying his face, he said a silent prayer. To have the courage to tell Lennie that her cousin was missing, Jamin would need all his strength.

Jamin walked into the living room to find Jace arguing with Daria about their bowling match the night before. Lennie interrupted to remind him there was no way to cheat.

"How is that even possible, Jace? It's just our arms, the balls, and the lanes. If anybody needs to cheat, it's your weak ass arm. Face it. You're officially the gutterball guru of this crew."

Their friends erupted in boisterous laughter. Before Jace could respond, Jamin cleared his throat. They all turned to face him. "Uhh hey, sorry to interrupt. But umm, Lennie ... I called everyone here because ..." His voice trailed off. This was harder than he could've imagined. He didn't want to be the one to tell her about Shayla. Jace stood from behind the small island bar. His best friend offered a nod of reassurance. Jamin's eyes went to the floor. He massaged the back of his neck. Lifting his head, Jamin cleared his throat again. "I uhh ... damn Lennie, there's no easy way to say this."

"Say what?" She cast Jace a curious glance before turning back to face Jamin.

Jamin lifted his shoulder in a half shrug and mumbled, "I don't know where Shayla is."

Lennie pushed the bar stool out and got up. She glanced around the room. "So, that's why we're here? And what do you mean, you don't know where she is?"

He forced a firm swallow to get rid of the boulder that appeared to have expanded in his throat. Jamin's shook his head from left to right quietly before sharing everything he'd told Jace. He finished, holding out his hands. "I swear there was nothing wrong with her last night when y'all left us. She didn't send a text to say she made it here, but I ain't think nothing of it. And I ain't got no missed calls. I know she wouldn't just go off on her own. I've checked and nothing's been touched or is missing ..." Jamin's eyes left Lennie's. He looked to his three friends and then his gaze settled back on her. He whispered. "'cept Shayla."

The deafening silence in the spacious room bounced off the walls. Lennie sat down. She leaned forward, resting her hands on her knees. Jamin observed the wrinkled lines forming in the middle of her forehead. Her eyes traveled up to meet his. Lennie shook her head vigorously. She straightened her posture and pointed to the front of his suite. "No. I saw her walk into this room last night."

Jamin's eyes darted over to Zayne and then to Jace. He'd had too much to drink the night before. Suddenly, the guilt weighed heavily on his shoulders. His voice was low. "I would've paid attention, but I crashed as soon as I came in. I didn't realize she wasn't here until I woke up. I was drinking and I—"

"No, don't do that." Jace objected, coming to stand at his side. "You didn't know, and you still don't know what's happened."

Zayne moved from around the island to stand on the other side of Jamin. He gripped Jamin's shoulder and squeezed. "Jace is right. We'll figure this out."

Jamin jerked away. "How? You got a plan? What about you? Y'all keep telling me to relax, but I can't. How can I? What are we supposed to do next?" His barrage of questions wasn't aimed solely at Zayne. He probed Jace and Daria while shifting his piercing gaze between the friends.

"Jay, give us a minute to think this through, okay? I ain't got nothing off the dome in this exact moment. But I know we will come up with something." Zayne reassured, clasping his hands together.

Daria's voice was low as she inquired, "Do we need to call the police at this point?"

"It ain't been twenty-four hours. They'll tell us to wait to file a missing person's report. I suggest we go down to the lobby and talk to security. Let 'em know what happened. Maybe they'll let us look at the cameras." Jace suggested.

Suddenly, Lennie hopped up, grabbing her bag from the island. She dug through it until she pulled out her cell. After swiping a few times, she released an audible sigh of relief. She twisted her head and smiled at Jamin. "She's still sharing her location."

Jamin's eyebrows shot up. He closed the distance between them. "Say what?"

"Her location. Me and Shay always keep our locations on." Lennie placed her phone down on the island. Everyone crowded around and focused their eyes on the device. She pointed and exclaimed, "And she's here in the hotel!"

"What the hell? Then why isn't she answering the phone?"

"That's what I'm about to find out." Lennie said, picking up the phone. She swiped the screen to start a FaceTime call with Shayla.

Jamin watched as the screen flashed Shayla's name. After a couple of trills, the call went to voicemail.

Lennie's face scrunched up, and she huffed. "I know the fuck she did not just ignore my call. Hang on." She tried calling again, but Shayla sent her to voicemail.

Lennie stared at her phone for a couple of beats. She snapped her finger. "I know what we can do. Let me put a call into Derrik's executive assistant."

The feeling of desperation had dissipated, but Jamin was now bothered by Shayla's motives for disappearing and ignoring their calls. While waiting for Lennie to finish on the phone, he lowered himself onto one of the bar stools. He thought about the day before and if there was anything that might have prompted Shayla to distance herself from everybody. Nothing was out of the ordinary. For the past week, their mornings consisted of passionate lovemaking, breakfast or brunch, and the activities he planned except the day before. With them performing tonight, they kept it simple and hung out with the crew. They were good until ... the lines of Jamin's forehead wrinkled. *Aneeka and Erwin!* The more he thought about it, Jamin realized Shayla was thrown off by their presence. Aneeka said something to Shayla that left her seething when they walked away. He didn't want to jump to conclusions, but he had a feeling her abrupt change in mood had to be from running into her former rival.

"Got it!" Lennie's voice interrupted Jamin from his train of thoughts. She hopped up from the bar stool and grabbed her bag. "Let's go. She's six floors down."

Jamin dashed to the bedroom. He grabbed the first pair of J's he saw in the closet and threw them on in a matter of seconds. Collecting his wallet, cell phone, and the card key for the room, he met up with everyone else in the hallway. As they made their way into the elevator he said, "In light of all of this, I'mma need her to share that location."

Lennie chuckled, "I thought y'all would've done that by now."

Once they reached the floor, everyone followed Jamin down the hall to the door of the room Lennie shared the number she was in. He rapped against the door softly.

Her voice was muffled behind the door. "Didn't you read the sign? I don't need anything."

"Shayla baby, this morning was real quiet without you. We've gotten so used to hearing you singing to us. Ahem, and heh Jimmy sure as hell missed waking up to you singing to him."

Jace's loud voice came from behind. "Jimmy? Who the fuck is Jimmy?"

Jamin turned his head to the side abruptly. He shot his best friend a menacing glare and mouthed 'shut the fuck up.'

"My bad, yo," Jace whispered, holding his hands up.

Shaking his head, Jamin leaned in closer to the door. "Baby, the last half an hour was some scary shit. I didn't know what happened to you. Waking up to an empty bed, then room, not hearing you, it really fucked your boy up." Jamin quickly glanced over his shoulder before clearing his throat. His voice was low. "Ohhh when you walk by …" He paused for a beat. Pressing a hand against the door, he started the song over and raised the pitch of his voice by a few octaves. Jamin heard when Jace whispered.

"Isn't that the song from the movie with whatchamacallit in there? What's his name? Chris Tucker played in it."

"*Rush Hour*?" Daria replied.

Zayne confirmed with an enthusiastic head nod. "Yep, that's it!"

"Hold up. I know this nigga ain't singing MiMi right now."

Jamin spun around and hissed. "If it's to get my baby to open the door, hell yea, I'mma sing MiMi. Now back me the fuck up!"

"I know that's right. If he don't, I got your back," Lennie said, rolling her eyes at Jace.

Zayne and Daria exchanged knowing nods with Jace when he turned to face them. Rocking his head back and forth, a full grin split his face, and Jace cheered. "You know I got you, Jay. Let's get your girl to open this door."

Jamin smiled, pivoting on his heel. He decided to sing Shayla's favorite song a few octaves louder now that he had their help. A crowd had begun to gather at the other end of the hall. Some of them took out their phones to capture the group singing the R&B song acapella. The room door cracked open by the time he reached the bridge where Mariah claimed to be in heaven with her boyfriend. Their eyes met. Shayla peered behind him and smiled. She joined them in singing the song's final chorus. The crowd that'd watched them broke out in applause.

"Hey songbird, we're glad to see you're okay. And don't worry Jay, we'll handle them." Jace gestured down the hall. "Hit us up when y'all are ready to link up."

"Now you know damn well after what Shay just put Jamin through, they ain't gonna hit nobody up until it's time for the show," Lennie said, shaking her head at him. She then smirked at Shayla and threw up the hand signal for her to call.

With a sheepish grin, Shayla tipped her head in agreement. Once they said their goodbyes to their friends and they headed in the direction of the crowd, Jamin pushed Shayla's room door all the way open. Stepping inside the suite, he shut it behind him and pulled her into his arms. He took a deep breath and inhaled the sweet scent of mango and coconut. Earlier that morning, he'd missed having her beside him. Jamin buried his face in her neck. Releasing a deep sigh, he lifted his head and peered down into her sienna-colored irises. He held her gaze as he declared. "This ain't no daydream or fantasy. I'm here and I ain't going nowhere. No more running away or cutting me off, okay?"

She opened her mouth to say something, but he didn't give her a chance to get it out. Jamin lowered his mouth to hers, sharing a passionate kiss that held nothing back. As he pulled her in closer, his fingers caressed her soft curves. Shayla moaned and arched her back in response to his touch, her body melding into his. He poured everything he had into the kiss, losing himself in her taste and her scent. Eventually, they broke apart, both breathing heavily. Jamin could feel his heart racing in his chest, and he knew that she could feel it, too. Now was the time to express his true feelings for her. He smiled, brushing the back of his hand down the side of her face. "Shayla baby, I ain't say it before when I should've. It's not like I ain't want to. I guess if anything, the moment wasn't right. Remember that night I told you about Cami, when I said life can be cruel, heartless, and unapologetic? You can never be ready to lose the people we love."

Shayla nodded.

"With this happening, I know now more than anything else, the beauty in life is when that unexpected moment love captures you. Love is the destiny when two people find each other without even looking. I love you. Do you hear me? I love you. So please, don't ever leave me like that again."

Shayla wrung her hands together. Bringing her tear-filled eyes up to meet his, she choked out. "Oh Jamin, I love you too. And I'm sorry. I-I just, I just needed a minute to … " She dropped her head.

Hooking a finger beneath her chin, Jamin raised her head. "Hey, hey look at me."

She pulled away, shaking her head. Shayla stepped back, buried her face in her hands, and started crying.

"No, baby, don't cry. There's no reason to." His voice had a firm yet loving tone.

Shayla shook her head, sobbing more. Jamin needed Shayla to trust and believe he had her back. He would never let anything bad happen to her. He gently grabbed her shoulders. Pulling her back to him, he kissed the top of her head before resting his chin there. She buried her face in his chest. He drew circles on her lower back as her sobs quieted down. "Listen, you don't have to go through this alone. You have me to lean on now. I'm gonna be here for you. Do you understand? We're gonna get through this together," he murmured softly.

Suddenly, Jamin felt her body stiffen. She lifted her head. Pinching her eyebrows together, her tear-stained face twisted into a confused expression. Shayla withdrew from his arms.

She wiped her face with the back of her hands. Her voice cracked. "Get through what? What is there to get through? Do you think something's wrong with me, Jamin?"

"Come here." Jamin gently took hold of her arm. He guided her over to the bed. The moment he sat on the firm mattress, Jamin frowned. Unlike their suite upstairs, the bedding in the room lacked the softness. Pushing the thought to the back of his mind, he focused on his woman and her luscious lips. They were poked out in frustration by what he'd said. He pulled Shayla onto his lap. His dick responded right away, pulsing and swelling against her softness. He'd missed her too. Giving the two plump cheeks a firm squeeze, Jamin took his time explaining what he meant. "No. I don't think nothing's wrong with you."

"Then why were you talking to me like that?" she whined.

Her eyes glistened as she stared up at him with puppy dog eyes. She blinked, and a couple of tears rolled down her cheeks. Using his thumb, he swiped them away. Jamin gathered her in a tight embrace. He kissed the moist saltiness on her cheeks. "Shayla baby, you didn't have to leave. You never have to run from me when something upsets you. Let me ask you something. Do you trust me?"

Her response was a silent nod.

Jamin held up a hand while shaking his head. "Nah, baby, it's important that I hear you say this. 'Cause what happened this morning can't happen again between us. Do you trust me?"

"Yes Jamin, I trust you."

"I'm not gon' let nobody fuck with my girl. We not gon' worry about shit from the past a'ight. And we shol' as hell ain't about to worry about no raggedy weave wearing chick named Akeela, whatever her name is or a nigga with *da white around his lips* named Erwin, popping up trying to throw shade your way either. My baby 'bout to do the damn thang tonight. You were born to sang, right?"

Shayla's eyes widened in surprise.

Jamin chuckled, shaking his head. "What? You thought I wouldn't figure this shit out? Your man pays close attention to everything about you. Ain't nothing was wrong until them two clowns showed up."

"So, you didn't think I ran away?" She laughed nervously.

He squeezed her tighter before responding. "Nah, baby. I was scared shitless and didn't know what to think. I panicked 'cause you wasn't answering your phone. You wasn't with Daria or Lennie and I knew you left with them last night. It didn't click until about thirty minutes ago when Lennie saw your location was on. Speaking of that, I'mma need you to share it." Jamin looked around the suite. "Matter of fact, where's your phone? We need to handle that right now. I'm dead serious. I'm not going through that again. My heart couldn't take that shit."

Shayla smiled and hopped up from his lap. She went over to the dresser on the other side of the suite to retrieve her phone from her bag. After handing it to Jamin, he quickly set up the Find My Friends app so they could keep track of one another. Suddenly Shayla began humming a familiar tune.

"If you call my name. Shayla Starr. Call me, text me if you wanna reach me. When you wanna FaceTime me, it's okay. Whenever you need me, Jay. I'll be on my way. Call me." She repeated the words, snapping her fingers and twirling around.

"The hell?" Jamin cocked his head to the side.

In the middle of a pirouette, Shayla stopped and groaned. She plopped down on the bed next to him and grabbed his arm. "Come on, Babe. You gotta know this one."

He thought he knew, but he couldn't quite put his finger on the tune. His eyebrows bunched together, and he held up his palms. "You got me, baby. I don't know."

"Ugh, how could you forget Kim Possible?" She pressed her lips together in a pout.

Jamin shook his head. He thought to himself she could be corny at times, but still sexy as hell. In a smooth movement, he scooped her up. Scooting to the middle of the bed, he eased Shayla onto her back. Jamin stretched out next to her and propped himself up on an elbow. With his other hand, he used his thumb to run across her bottom lip. Her lips were like sweet cushions as he leaned over, crushing his lips against them. Shayla's moan vibrated in between their mouths. She started grinding against his now rock-hard erection. He eased from their kiss and smirked.

"What?" she questioned with a puzzled expression.

Jamin dropped his gaze between them. He gripped his hardened shaft and replied in a low, husky voice as he raised his eyes to meet hers. "How about you do a duet with Jimmy? He missed you singing for him this morning."

EPILOGUE

Nine months later...

"Hey, y'all! Heeeeeey! What's happening? Welcome to another episode of *Baller Bizness* with yours truly, LaLa."

"Annnnd your lovely co-host, Sisko!"

LaLa twisted her head in the direction of a different camera. "If you're just tuning in, you're tardy for one helluva party."

"No, if you're in the A and not here at the Mercedes Benz stadium with us, you're missing out on one of the city's most anticipated events of the year." Sisko interjected with a neckroll.

LaLa snapped her fingers. "Facts! I've been amped about this weekend for months. I couldn't wait to show off this fit."

"Sheesh LaLa, I'm loving this cinched blazer, the leather corset, and shorts. No, how about these thigh-high red bottom boots? It's giving bad and boujee anchor vibes. I see you, boo!"

She took a step back and did a quick shimmy shake. "Why, thank you, Sisko. But I know you're not talking. Who's out here showing them how to rock Tom Ford the right way, hmm?"

"Who, me?" Sisko pressed a hand to his chest. Then he twirled and did a fashion catwalk that garnered a standing ovation from the fans nearby. "Oh, y'all hush!" Sisko waved them off and pursed his lips.

LaLa laughed heartily. "Stop being modest. The people know you're going to slay. But when I tell y'all your fellow ATLiens showed out, they didn't come to play. Derrik said tonight's theme was *Bad & Boujee*. Ha! That's all we've seen tonight. The men and women of Hotlanta put on for their city. When I say the energy in here is on ten. Whew! If you're catching it 'cause you're watching somebody's IG live or seeing snippets from their stories, that ain't the same."

Sisko rocked his head from side to side. "Nope! It don't even come close." He gestured towards the floor. "Y'all gotta be in here to feel this. I think I feel the floor vibrating."

LaLa nodded in agreement. "Most definitely. It's a vibe. The ATLiens have been here since the doors opened at 6:00pm. And for this special episode of *Baller Bizness*, we're coming to you live and direct with our behind-the-scenes access. We've been bringing the viewers exclusive interviews from some of BlakBeatz's hottest artists. To think, the night's just beginning." LaLa paused for a beat and turned to face Sisko.

He smiled, popping his lips. "If you haven't been to a BlakBeatz's R&B Experience, you're missing out. We've already had the night begin with some ahh-mazing performances from the label's artists." Sisko fanned himself. "Did you see G-Weezy? I don't know if a man can get any finer than that one right there."

"Now you know that man is already spoken for. Don't let his wife Monica snatch you up. She don't play about G."

"Hmph, I wouldn't either." Sisko waved dismissively. "But anyway, who we got up next?"

"I've been waiting for this group. They've turned into my absolute fave this past year. Talk about how you spoke this right into existence."

He snickered and moistened his lips. "I know I've got the power of the tongue, but what are you talking 'bout?"

LaLa shot a blank stare at Sisko before shaking her head.

His lips were puckered. He batted his lashes and sassed. "What?"

"Nothing. As I was getting ready to say, you mentioned that they were gonna need to bring in a powerhouse voice and she must be able to deal with Jamin Love."

"Oooh, yes! Now I remember." Sisko started clapping.

Lala flashed a knowing smile as she continued. "In the last year, we've watched Love in Minor Keyz better known as LMK, once again top the charts with their eclectic, smooth, and soulful sounds. Tragically, the band lost its cherished lead singer, Cami Love, a little more than two years ago. The band would return after taking a break to mourn their loss but struggle a bit to find someone who could fill a role that, of course, could never be replaced. When so many counted them out, me included, Jamin Love and his friends would prove that life's about facing unexpected challenges and setbacks. They weren't facing a defeat."

"LMK said what y'all thought. We wasn't coming back? Heh, we back and we ain't going nowhere!" Sisko cheered.

"Yes, yes, and from an exclusive interview with Jamin, he said, *the melodies carry on even after the song is over.* Mmhmm, after sitting down with him, didn't you feel how much he loves music?"

Sisko bobbed his head in agreement. "I know he does, but there's someone else he loves just as much as music that I'm looking forward to hearing. Can we skip to the good part?"

"Since my co-host is losing patience, y'all, let me move this right along. LMK wasn't immune to the difficulties that come with replacing a member in their crew. Like others in the business, they too had their fair share of dealing with a revolving door of singers who didn't work out. That is until they came across the incomparable Shayla Starr."

"My girl!" Sisko pumped his fist.

LaLa shook her head. "As y'all can see, he's a fan. Like always, Derrik Carter found another hidden gem and signed Shayla to BlakBeatz becoming LMK's lead vocalist. They released their fourth album *Soundz of a Good Tyme* which earned a Grammy for Best Urban Contemporary Album and *Crazy for Your Love* as Song of the Year. Please put your hands together and welcome to the stage, Love in Minor Keyz or as we all know them, L-M-K!"

The room was pitch dark as the lights dimmed, and a sea of colored strobes bounced off the walls. Out of nowhere, five figures appeared onstage – LMK – and settled into their respective places with amps, guitars, and drum sets ready. The crowd erupted in cheers and clapping that made the floor rumble under

Jamin's feet. He sat at the baby grand piano, raised his hands in the air, and gave a dazzling smile while keying the opening chords of their set.

"LMK, it's time to give the people what they want."

"And what they want?" Shayla, Jace, Daria, and Zayne responded in unison.

Jamin's velvety tenor voice murmured, "All of this L-O-V-E."

For the next half an hour, the group performed a few songs from their earlier catalog and finished the show with the chart toppers from their current album. When the last song ended, Shayla began to walk off the stage.

"Shayla baby, hang on." Jamin called out to her. He leaned towards the microphone. "We have an encore performance for the people."

Shayla gave him a look, indicating she had no idea what was going on. This was exactly what Jamin was counting on. He didn't explain, but instead motioned for her to come back to where she'd been standing in the middle of the stage. Once he saw her there, he winked and nodded to his friends and bandmates. Soon after, the stage lights were lowered.

Jamin began playing the familiar notes and belting in his smooth tenor voice. "Ooooh, baby ..."

The audience exploded into cheers and claps when Jamin's bandmates joined him in singing the famous Prince song they chose to cover. Jamin meant every word they were singing. He would always be there for her, no matter what happened, even until the end of time. She now had his heart and mind as if it was her own property; he could go blind, but still be able to see her. Just like Prince said in the song, there were no words to describe how much she meant to him. Not even the word "love" could express it fully.

"I knew you were it for me, Shayla baby. You weren't trying to hear it though." Jamin twisted his head to speak to the audience. "She ain't wanna be a runner for your boy."

Shayla mouthed the word 'nope.'

Jamin flashed her a grin and continued rapping to the beat. "Was you scared, girl? Nah, you was just playing hard to get. One thing was for certain, I was gon' be yo fantasy. Check it y'all, it didn't take long before those sexy lips were singing a different tune."

Forever and always,
I'll be your shining star.
With you, I'll spend my days,
No matter where we are.
Our love will never fade,
It will only grow stronger.
Until the end of time,
Our love will last longer.

The spotlight was on Jamin when the stage lights abruptly went off. His smooth fingers glided across the keys in unison as his soulful playing enveloped the room in seduction. Every keystroke expressing a feeling, and every note was a representation of that emotion. The music swelled and built up to a crescendo, ripping through the room with a raw intensity. Jamin bellowed out the last hook as the lights illuminated the stage behind him.

With you, I am complete,
My heart is yours to keep.
Through thick and thin,
Our love will never dim.
You are my everything,
My reason to sing.
I truly love you,
And I'll always be true.
Love is too weak to define,
Just what you mean to me.

The crowd erupted into thunderous applause when he finished. Jamin rose from the piano. His eyes never left hers as he made his way over to where Shayla stood. She was sobbing and nodding vigorously by the time he reached her.

Jamin gathered her into his arms. "What are you nodding for? I ain't asked you nothing yet, baby."

She playfully pushed his chest and pointed to the bright lights on the stage. He glanced in the direction of her outstretched finger.

SHAYLA BABY, WILL YOU MARRY ME?

"Oh that. Nah, I need to hear you say it. But lemme do this right." Jamin quickly went down on his knee. He reached behind his back and pulled out a black velvet box. "My heart races with emotion and happiness as I'm here before you and all these people pledging my love. You are the most remarkable person to ever enter my life, and I can't fathom my existence without you in it. When we first met, I knew there was something special about us. Your love and kindness have given me unending courage, and I am infinitely thankful for you. I want to spend the rest of my life with you, growing and learning together. I promise to love you, cherish you, and support you always. You are the missing piece of my heart, and I cannot wait to spend forever with you. He finally echoed the words, "Shayla baby, will you marry me?"

"Yes! Yes!" she squealed. Tears of joy ran down her cheeks as Jamin slid the ring onto her finger.

Scrambling to his feet, Jamin opened his arms to her, and she leaped into them. He hugged her tightly and whispered, "I love you so much."

She cried, "I love you too, Jamin!"

They stood in a tight embrace for what seemed like an eternity. When Jamin heard Jace's loud, boisterous laugh, it was then that he remembered the crowd that had gathered around them, each cheering and clapping.

"Let's get out of here," Jamin said, and Shayla nodded in agreement.

He led her through the crowd, his arm around her waist, protecting her from the throng of people that were trying to congratulate them. They made their way backstage, where Jamin had a surprise waiting for Shayla. He had rented an SUV to take them to a luxury hotel where they would spend the night as an engaged couple.

Once they were inside, Jamin pulled Shayla close to him and kissed her passionately. His hands roamed over her body. Shayla moaned softly. As their kiss deepened, Jamin pulled Shayla onto his lap, pressing his hard erection against her pelvis.

"I want you now," Jamin whispered into her ear, his voice husky with need.

Shayla nodded. Gently, Jamin placed Shayla on the luxurious leather seats, his hands exploring her body as he showered her with fervent kisses. He was quick and efficient as he removed his own clothes, followed by hers. Soon, her voluptuous curves were exposed under the gentle illumination of the limousine. She arched her back when Jamin's lips found one of her erect diamonds. He sucked it into his mouth while his hand roamed over her other breast.

Jamin's other hand slipped between her legs, parting her to his touch. He slid his fingers into her moist heat, and she moaned when he found her clit and began massaging it. Jamin lifted his head from her breast and kissed her deeply. His fingers worked their magic, and Shayla began to writhe beneath him.

"Jamin!" she cried out. "I'm … I'm gonna … shhhhhit!"

He rotated his fingers, pumping harder and faster until she cried out in release, her back arching off the seat as she came in his hand. He removed his fingers and licked them clean, reveling in her flavor.

"Mmhmm, I love the way you taste."

Jamin then pushed her knees up and wedged himself between her thighs. He pressed the tip of his throbbing erection against her wet entrance. Shayla wrapped her hand around the shaft and began stroking him as he entered her. Even after months of being together, his fiancée's pussy was still deliciously tight. He smirked at the new title. *My fiancée.*

"Ohhh babe … it feels like … like you're stretching me out!"

He leaned down and kissed her, feeling the warmth of her breath on his face. Her lips were soft, and she opened them for him, inviting him to explore the dark heat of her mouth. She wrapped her arms around his neck and pulled him down so that their bodies melded into one flesh. Her velvet cage tightened around his shaft. Jamin's groans were echoed by Shayla as they began to move in unison. He plunged into her deep and pistoned fast. She met him thrust for thrust, crying out in pleasure. He dug his fingers into Shayla's hips as his thrusts became more powerful and wild, every caress sending her higher until she climaxed with a loud scream.

"Yes! Yes! Oh god, yes!"

Watching her unravel, Jamin could no longer fight his own release. His balls were tightening. He gritted his teeth against the need to explode building within. He stiffened and convulsed. His thick seed spurted into her womb, where it mixed with her juices and dribbled out over his balls.

"Ffffuck!"

A moment later, he rolled off, his spent shaft still twitching. Jamin fell back against the seat, panting. Shayla sat up and crawled into his arms. She lay on his chest with her head tucked under his chin. He draped an arm around her, squeezing her closer.

Shayla gazed into Jamin's eyes, overwhelmed with emotion. "I never thought I'd be so lucky. I love you, Jamin," she whispered.

Jamin pressed his hot lips against hers and kissed her with a passion that seemed greater than life itself. "And I love you, Shayla baby. You're mine now, forever and ever."

This was love in a major chord—loud and powerful.

Thank You

Thank you so much for reading! I ask whether you enjoyed this story or not, to please consider leaving a review wherever you purchased this book and/or mark it as read on Goodreads. I also hate errors, but they do happen. If you catch any, please send them to the publisher directly at info@flamesentertain.com with ERRORS as the subject.

Afterword

'*And my man, thank you to my man*' was all I could hear as I was getting closer to the end of this story. Shayla was yelling it the loudest in her Latto voice. Could you blame her after snagging Jamin? Wasn't he dreamy? He had me swooning a few times. I don't know how Shayla held out for as long as she did—being around him daily with his imposing body invading her space and having to inhale the same air that smelled so good. No wonder the poor girl had to keep a change of panties in her bookbag. Then once they got together, he was giving that good Vitamin D with soak baths included to keep her pH balanced. He even fed her the best French toast she'd ever had. And let's not forget about that stir fry dinner he whipped up once he took the trash out. Right. Thank you to my man! But that's Jamin expressing his love language to the woman that's deserving of it. Besides, he couldn't deny being totally smitten once meeting his songbird, Shayla baby. Despite his gruff exterior, she had him caught up from day one. Likewise, Shayla was just as gone as Jamin with her attraction for the sexy grouch. Once he finally opened up to share what happened to his cousin, Cami and Shayla told him she would do everything to be the light he needed. I knew it was a sealed deal. I was so happy when they got out of their own way and welcomed the love that they both deserved to receive from each other. To know they're going to be making love songs together for years to come makes my heart happy. That proposal though. And doing it with a cover to Prince's *Adore*? Whew! Again, thank you to my man!

I'm sure I don't have to tell you that I had a lot of fun penning this story. The idea for Jamin and the Love in Minor series came to me during a writing sprint with my Penning Valley group late last year. I was working on the storyline while promoting The Enough Series. I can remember that a major shift in the storyline happened after a visit to Black Coffee Atlanta earlier this year. If you've been following me, then you know about the signing events I've had there. During my first event in March, I had the pleasure of meeting two of its founders, Jamin Butler and Christopher Bolden. They shared a little bit of history about The Black Coffee Company and how this coffee shop came to be. I'm not going to front y'all, I was proud of and inspired by these five friends—Black men—who pooled their financial resources together to launch this company to sell organic coffee beans and branded merchandise to create resources and opportunities for their communities.

What I have to share is some of the real-life inspiration behind the characters: Jamin, Jace, and Shayla that came while I visited Black Coffee. I'm always people watching for research and inspiration. Sometimes I meet character muses for my stories. For example, while I was getting the table display set up, Jamin came over to introduce himself and welcome me to Black Coffee. I'm like wait a minute your name sounds like my main character, Waymon in the story I'm working on right now, but I love your name better. The fact that you have locs just like him, I think I'm going to change his name. He tells me "Well, you should know it has a biblical meaning. Make sure you look up what it means later when you get a chance." I take note of that and continue with getting my table ready. Later in the day I ended up meeting the character muses for Shayla and Jace. By the time I left Black Coffee I had several updates for Love in A Minor. When I got around to looking up Jamin's name later that evening, I was blown away. So, it means, *"right hand"* and is a reminder to the namesake of the importance of honor and loyalty to the people they love. We saw how Jamin Love was about the people closest to him. Need I say more?

I want to say thank you, Black Coffee Atlanta for allowing me the space for a signing event. That day will always be one of my most cherished moments. Who knew after hearing the story of how Black Coffee came to be and spending the day there to experience the culture and vibe, it would've inspired so much in what I've penned to be one of my favorite love stories. I appreciate your continued support. You already know, it's forever mutual!

Of course, a special thanks goes out to Jamin Butler for allowing me to use your name. When you said to look up the meaning, I knew it was nothing short of kismet on how everything tied together for my main character, his friends, and this story. I hope I made you and Ayron smile big with this one.

Now, I'm sure you're all wondering, who's up next. If you hadn't figured it out—Lennie and Jace of course! Those two with all that bantering back and forth. We need to see if their situationship moves into something more serious. We also need to know if the girls get away with setting the guys up in that bowling rematch. Lennie was dead serious about that new Birkin bag. If you'd like a sneak peek of what's to come with Lennie and Jace, check out this bonus scene: https://bit.ly/3ttg98v. Stay tuned, **Love in B Minor** is coming Spring 2024!

Also by Mo Flames

<u>Enough Series</u>
One Ain't Enough
One Still Ain't Enough
One Is Enough

<u>Infinity Series</u>
Make You Mine

Girl, He Don't Want Your Ass,
The 10 Signs He's Not Interested (Non-Fiction)

About the Author

Mo Flames is an avid reader, writer, wine lover and a super fan of The Office. She pens contemporary romance stories with complex characters, controversial topics, and unpredictable plot twists. Mo's experiences and creativity fuel her written words. She's never been bashful about racy relationship topics. She's unashamed and unapologetically real. It echoes with her tagline, 'leaving that fire between the sheets, literally.'

When she's not writing, she enjoys playing the Sims, reading romance and suspense, binge watching The Office, Snapped, Criminal Minds or any crime television shows. She resides in Atlanta, GA with her husband and daughter.

Make sure you connect with Mo!

https://linktr.ee/moflames

Made in the USA
Columbia, SC
06 June 2024

36586247R00124